I0749238

Victorian Short Stories of Troubled Marriages

Rudyard Kipling, Ella D'Arcy, et al.

Victorian Short Stories of Troubled Marriages

The present edition is a reproduction of previous publication of this classic work. Minor typographical errors may have been corrected without note; however, for an authentic reading experience the spelling, punctuation, and capitalization have been retained from the original text.

ISBN: 978-1-64799-946-9

CONTENTS

THE BRONCKHORST DIVORCE-CASE
By Rudyard Kipling

(Civil and Military Gazette, 26 September 1884)

In the daytime, when she moved about me,
  In the night, when she was sleeping at my side,—
I was wearied, I was wearied of her presence,
Day by day and night by night I grew to hate her—
  Would God that she or I had died!
—CONFESSIONS

There was a man called Bronckhorst—a three-cornered, middle-aged man in the Army—grey as a badger, and, some people said, with a touch of country-blood in him. That, however, cannot be proved. Mrs. Bronckhorst was not exactly young, though fifteen years younger than her husband. She was a large, pale, quiet woman, with heavy eyelids over weak eyes, and hair that turned red or yellow as the lights fell on it.

Bronckhorst was not nice in any way. He had no respect for the pretty public and private lies that make life a little less nasty than it is. His manner towards his wife was coarse. There are many things—including actual assault with the clenched fist—that a wife will endure; but seldom a wife can bear—as Mrs. Bronckhorst bore—with a long course of brutal, hard chaff, making light of her weaknesses, her headaches, her small fits of gaiety, her dresses, her queer little attempts to make herself attractive to her husband when she knows that she is not what she has been, and—worst of all—the love that she spends on her children. That particular sort of heavy-handed jest was specially dear to Bronckhorst. I suppose that he had first slipped into it, meaning no harm, in the honeymoon, when folk find their ordinary stock of endearments run short, and so go to the other extreme to express their feelings. A similar impulse makes a man say, 'Hutt, you old beast!' when a favourite horse nuzzles his coat-front. Unluckily, when the reaction of marriage sets in, the form of speech remains, and, the tenderness having died out, hurts the wife more than she cares to say. But Mrs. Bronckhorst was devoted to her 'Teddy' as she called him. Perhaps that was why he objected to her. Perhaps—this is only a theory to account for his infamous behaviour later on—he gave way to the queer, savage feeling that sometimes takes by the throat a husband twenty years married, when he sees, across the table, the same, same face of his wedded wife, and knows that, as he has sat facing it, so must he continue to sit until the day of its death or his own. Most men and all women know the spasm. It only lasts for three breaths as a rule, must be a 'throw-back' to times when men and women were rather worse than they are now, and is too unpleasant to be discussed.

Dinner at the Bronckhorsts' was an infliction few men cared to undergo. Bronckhorst took a pleasure in saying things that made his wife wince. When their little boy came in at dessert Bronckhorst used to give him half a glass of wine, and, naturally enough, the poor little mite got first riotous, next miserable, and was removed screaming. Bronckhorst asked if that was the way Teddy usually behaved, and whether Mrs. Bronckhorst could not spare some of her time 'to teach the little beggar decency'. Mrs. Bronckhorst, who loved the boy more than her own life, tried not to cry—her spirit seemed to have been broken by her marriage. Lastly, Bronckhorst used to say, 'There! That'll do, that'll do. For God's sake try to behave like a rational woman. Go into the drawing-room.' Mrs. Bronckhorst would go, trying to carry it all off with a smile; and the guest of the evening would feel angry and uncomfortable.

After three years of this cheerful life—for Mrs. Bronckhorst had no women-friends to talk to—the station was startled by the news that Bronckhorst had instituted proceedings on the criminal count, against a man called Biel, who certainly had been rather attentive to Mrs. Bronckhorst whenever she had appeared in public. The utter want of reserve with which Bronckhorst treated his own dishonour helped us to know that the evidence against Biel would be entirely circumstantial and native. There were no letters; but Bronckhorst said openly that he would rack Heaven and Earth until he saw Biel superintending the manufacture of carpets in the Central Jail. Mrs. Bronckhorst kept entirely to her house, and let charitable folks say what they pleased. Opinions were divided. Some two-thirds of the station jumped at once to the conclusion that Biel was guilty; but a dozen men who knew and liked him held by him. Biel was furious and surprised. He denied the whole thing, and vowed that he would thrash Bronckhorst within an inch of his life. No jury, we knew, would convict a man on the criminal count on native evidence in a land where you can buy a murder-charge, including the corpse, all complete for fifty-four rupees; but Biel did not care to scrape through by the benefit of a doubt. He wanted the whole thing cleared; but, as he said one night, 'He can prove anything with servants' evidence, and I've only my bare word.' This was almost a month before the case came on; and beyond agreeing with Biel, we could do little. All that we could be sure of was that the native evidence would be bad enough to blast Biel's character for the rest of his service; for when a native begins perjury he perjures himself thoroughly. He does not boggle over details.

Some genius at the end of the table whereat the affair was being talked over, said, 'Look here! I don't believe lawyers are any good. Get a man to wire to Strickland, and beg him to come down and pull us through.'

Strickland was about a hundred and eighty miles up the line. He had not long been married to Miss Youghal, but he scented in the telegram a chance of return to the old detective work that his soul lusted after, and next time he came in and heard our story. He finished his pipe and said oracularly, 'We must get at the evidence. Oorya bearer, Mussulman khit and sweeper ayah, I suppose, are the pillars of the charge. I am on in this piece; but I'm afraid I'm getting rusty in my talk.'

He rose and went into Biel's bedroom, where his trunk had been put, and shut the door. An hour later, we heard him say, 'I hadn't the heart to part with my old make-ups when I married. Will this do?' There was a loathly fakir salaaming in the doorway.

'Now lend me fifty rupees,' said Strickland, 'and give me your Words of
Honour that you won't tell my wife.'

He got all that he asked for, and left the house while the table drank his health. What he did only he himself knows. A fakir hung about Bronckhorst's compound for twelve days. Then a sweeper appeared, and when Biel heard of him, he said that Strickland was an angel full-fledged. Whether the sweeper made love to Janki, Mrs. Bronckhorst's ayah, is a question which concerns Strickland exclusively.

He came back at the end of three weeks, and said quietly, 'You spoke the truth, Biel. The whole business is put up from beginning to end. Jove! It almost astonishes me! That Bronckhorst beast isn't fit to live.'

There was uproar and shouting, and Biel said, 'How are you going to prove it? You can't say that you've been trespassing on Bronckhorst's compound in disguise!'

'No,' said Strickland. 'Tell your lawyer-fool, whoever he is, to get up something strong about "inherent improbabilities" and "discrepancies of evidence". He won't have to speak, but it will make him happy, I'm going to run this business.'

Biel held his tongue, and the other men waited to see what would happen. They trusted Strickland as men trust quiet men. When the case came off the Court was crowded. Strickland hung about in the veranda of the Court, till he met the Mohammedan khitmutgar. Then he murmured a fakir's blessing in his ear, and asked him how his second wife did. The man spun round, and, as he looked into the eyes of 'Estreekin Sahib', his jaw dropped. You must remember that before Strickland was married, he was, as I have told you already, a power among natives. Strickland whispered a rather coarse vernacular proverb to the effect that he was abreast of all that was going on, and went into the Court armed with a gut trainer's-whip.

The Mohammedan was the first witness, and Strickland beamed upon him from the back of the Court. The man moistened his lips with his tongue and, in his abject fear of 'Estreekin Sahib', the fakir went back on every detail of his evidence—said he was a poor man, and God was his witness that he had forgotten everything that Bronckhorst Sahib had told him to say. Between his terror of Strickland, the Judge, and Bronckhorst he collapsed weeping.

Then began the panic among the witnesses. Janki, the ayah, leering chastely behind her veil, turned grey, and the bearer left the Court. He said that his Mamma was dying, and that it was not wholesome for any man to lie unthriftily in the presence of 'Estreekin Sahib'.

Biel said politely to Bronckhorst, 'Your witnesses don't seem to work. Haven't you any forged letters to produce?' But

Bronckhorst was swaying to and fro in his chair, and there was a dead pause after Biel had been called to order.

Bronckhorst's Counsel saw the look on his client's face, and without more ado pitched his papers on the little green-baize table, and mumbled something about having been misinformed. The whole Court applauded wildly, like soldiers at a theatre, and the Judge began to say what he thought.

*****

Biel came out of the Court, and Strickland dropped a gut trainer's-whip in the veranda. Ten minutes later, Biel was cutting Bronckhorst into ribbons behind the old Court cells, quietly and without scandal. What was left of Bronckhorst was sent home in a carriage; and his wife wept over it and nursed it into a man again. Later on, after Biel had managed to hush up the counter-charge against Bronckhorst of fabricating false evidence, Mrs. Bronckhorst, with her faint, watery smile, said that there had been a mistake, but it wasn't her Teddy's fault altogether. She would wait till her Teddy came back to her. Perhaps he had grown tired of her, or she had tried his patience, and perhaps we wouldn't cut her any more, and perhaps the mothers would let their children play with 'little Teddy' again. He was so lonely. Then the station invited Mrs. Bronckhorst everywhere, until Bronckhorst was fit to appear in public, when he went Home and took his wife with him. According to latest advices, her Teddy did come back to her, and they are moderately happy. Though, of course, he can never forgive her the thrashing that she was the indirect means of getting for him.

*****

What Biel wants to know is, 'Why didn't I press home the charge against the Bronckhorst brute, and have him run in?'

What Mrs. Strickland wants to know is, 'How did my husband bring such a lovely, lovely Waler from your station? I know all his money affairs; and I'm certain he didn't buy it.'

What I want to know is, 'How do women like Mrs. Bronckhorst come to marry men like Bronckhorst?'

And my conundrum is the most unanswerable of the three.

IRREMEDIABLE
By Ella D'Arcy

(Monochromes, London: John Lane, 1893)

A young man strolled along a country road one August evening after a long delicious day—a day of that blessed idleness the man of leisure never knows: one must be a bank clerk forty-nine weeks out of the fifty-two before one can really appreciate the exquisite enjoyment of doing nothing for twelve hours at a stretch. Willoughby had spent the morning lounging about a sunny rickyard; then, when the heat grew unbearable, he had retreated to an orchard, where, lying on his back in the long cool grass, he had traced the pattern of the apple-leaves diapered above him upon the summer sky; now that the heat of the day was over he had come to roam whither sweet fancy led him, to lean over gates, view the prospect, and meditate upon the pleasures of a well-spent day. Five such days had already passed over his head, fifteen more remained to him. Then farewell to freedom and clean country air! Back again to London and another year's toil.

He came to a gate on the right of the road. Behind it a footpath meandered up over a grassy slope. The sheep nibbling on its summit cast long shadows down the hill almost to his feet. Road and fieldpath were equally new to him, but the latter offered greener attractions; he vaulted lightly over the gate and had so little idea he was taking thus the first step towards ruin that he began to whistle 'White Wings' from pure joy of life.

The sheep stopped feeding and raised their heads to stare at him from pale-lashed eyes; first one and then another broke into a startled run, until there was a sudden woolly stampede of the entire flock. When Willoughby gained the ridge from which they had just scattered, he came in sight of a woman sitting on a stile at the further end of the field. As he advanced towards her he saw that she was young, and that she was not what is called 'a lady'—of which he was glad: an earlier episode in his career having indissolubly associated in his mind ideas of feminine refinement with those of feminine treachery.

He thought it probable this girl would be willing to dispense with the formalities of an introduction, and that he might venture with her on some pleasant foolish chat.

As she made no movement to let him pass he stood still, and, looking at her, began to smile.

She returned his gaze from unabashed dark eyes, and then laughed, showing teeth white, sound, and smooth as split hazelnuts.

'Do you wanter get over?' she remarked familiarly.

'I'm afraid I can't without disturbing you.'

'Dontcher think you're much better where you are?' said the girl, on which Willoughby hazarded:

'You mean to say looking at you? Well, perhaps I am!'

The girl at this laughed again, but nevertheless dropped herself down into the further field; then, leaning her arms upon the cross-bar, she informed the young man: 'No, I don't wanter spoil your walk. You were goin' p'raps ter Beacon Point? It's very pretty that wye.'

'I was going nowhere in particular,' he replied; 'just exploring, so to speak. I'm a stranger in these parts.'

'How funny! Imer stranger here too. I only come down larse Friday to stye with a Naunter mine in Horton. Are you stying in Horton?'

Willoughby told her he was not in Orton, but at Povey Cross Farm out in the other direction.

'Oh, Mrs. Payne's, ain't it? I've heard aunt speak ovver. She takes summer boarders, don't chee? I egspeck you come from London, heh?'

'And I expect you come from London too?' said Willoughby, recognizing the familiar accent.

'You're as sharp as a needle,' cried the girl with her unrestrained laugh; 'so I do. I'm here for a hollerday 'cos I was so done up with the work and the hot weather. I don't look as though I'd bin ill, do I? But I was, though: for it was just stiflin' hot up in our workrooms all larse month, an' tailorin's awful hard work at the bester times.'

Willoughby felt a sudden accession of interest in her. Like many intelligent young men, he had dabbled a little in Socialism, and at one time had wandered among the dispossessed; but since then, had caught up and held loosely the new doctrine—it is a good and fitting thing that woman also should earn her bread by the sweat of her brow. Always in reference to the woman who, fifteen months before, had treated him ill; he had said to himself that even the breaking of stones in the road should be considered a more feminine employment than the breaking of hearts.

He gave way therefore to a movement of friendliness for this working daughter of the people, and joined her on the other side of the stile in token of his approval. She, twisting round to face him, leaned now with her back against the bar, and the sunset fires lent a fleeting glory to her face. Perhaps she guessed how becoming the light was, for she took off her hat and let it touch to gold the ends and fringes of her rough abundant hair. Thus and at this moment she made an agreeable picture, to which stood as background all the beautiful, wooded Southshire view.

'You don't really mean to say you are a tailoress?' said Willoughby, with a sort of eager compassion.

'I do, though! An' I've bin one ever since I was fourteen. Look at my fingers if you don't b'lieve me.'

She put out her right hand, and he took hold of it, as he was expected to do. The finger-ends were frayed and blackened by needle-pricks, but the hand itself was plump, moist, and not unshapely. She meanwhile examined Willoughby's fingers enclosing hers.

'It's easy ter see you've never done no work!' she said, half admiring, half envious. 'I s'pose you're a tip-top swell, ain't you?'

'Oh, yes! I'm a tremendous swell indeed!' said Willoughby, ironically. He thought of his hundred and thirty pounds' salary; and he mentioned his position in the British and Colonial Banking house, without shedding much illumination on her mind, for she insisted:

'Well, anyhow, you're a gentleman. I've often wished I was a lady. It must be so nice ter wear fine clo'es an' never have ter do any work all day long.'

Willoughby thought it innocent of the girl to say this; it reminded him of his own notion as a child—that kings and queens put on their crowns the first thing on rising in the morning. His cordiality rose another degree.

'If being a gentleman means having nothing to do,' said he, smiling, 'I can certainly lay no claim to the title. Life isn't all beer and skittles with me, any more than it is with you. Which is the better reason for enjoying the present moment, don't you think? Suppose, now, like a kind little girl, you were to show me the way to Beacon Point, which you say is so pretty?'

She required no further persuasion. As he walked beside her through the upland fields where the dusk was beginning to fall, and the white evening moths to emerge from their daytime hiding-places, she asked him many personal questions, most of which he thought fit to parry. Taking no offence thereat, she told him, instead, much concerning herself and her family. Thus he learned her name was Esther Stables, that she and her people lived Whitechapel way; that her father was seldom sober, and her mother always ill; and that the aunt with whom she was staying kept the post-office and general shop in Orton village. He learned, too, that Esther was discontented with life in general; that, though she hated being at home, she found the country dreadfully dull; and that, consequently, she was extremely glad to have made his acquaintance. But what he chiefly realized when they parted was that he had spent a couple of pleasant hours talking nonsense with a girl who was natural, simple-minded, and entirely free from that repellently protective atmosphere with which a woman of the 'classes' so carefully surrounds herself. He and Esther had 'made friends' with the ease and rapidity of children before they have learned the dread meaning of 'etiquette', and they said good night, not without some talk of meeting each other again.

Obliged to breakfast at a quarter to eight in town, Willoughby was always luxuriously late when in the country, where he took his meals also in leisurely fashion, often reading from a book propped up on the table before him. But the morning after his meeting with Esther Stables found him less disposed to read than usual. Her image obtruded itself upon the printed page, and at length grew so importunate he came to the conclusion the only way to lay it was to confront it with the girl herself.

Wanting some tobacco, he saw a good reason for going into Orton. Esther had told him he could get tobacco and everything else at her aunt's. He found the post-office to be one of the first houses in the widely spaced village street. In front of the cottage was a small garden ablaze with old-fashioned flowers; and in a large garden at one side were apple-trees, raspberry and currant bushes, and six thatched beehives on a bench. The bowed windows of the little shop were partly screened by sunblinds; nevertheless the lower panes still displayed a heterogeneous collection of goods—lemons, hanks of yarn, white linen buttons upon blue cards, sugar cones, churchwarden pipes, and tobacco jars. A letter-box opened its narrow mouth low down in one wall, and over the door swung the sign, 'Stamps and money-order office', in black letters on white enamelled iron.

The interior of the shop was cool and dark. A second glass-door at the back permitted Willoughby to see into a small sitting-room, and out again through a low and square-paned window to the sunny landscape beyond. Silhouetted against the light were the heads of two women; the rough young head of yesterday's Esther, the lean outline and bugled cap of Esther's aunt.

It was the latter who at the jingling of the doorbell rose from her work and came forward to serve the customer; but the girl, with much mute meaning in her eyes, and a finger laid upon her smiling mouth, followed behind. Her aunt heard her footfall. 'What do you want here, Esther?' she said with thin disapproval; 'get back to your sewing.'

Esther gave the young man a signal seen only by him and slipped out into the side-garden, where he found her when his purchases were made. She leaned over the privet-hedge to intercept him as he passed.

'Aunt's an awful ole maid,' she remarked apologetically; 'I b'lieve she'd never let me say a word to enny one if she could help it.'

'So you got home all right last night?' Willoughby inquired; 'what did your aunt say to you?'

'Oh, she arst me where I'd been, and I tolder a lotter lies.' Then, with a woman's intuition, perceiving that this speech jarred, Esther made haste to add, 'She's so dreadful hard on me. I dursn't tell her I'd been with a gentleman or she'd never have let me out alone again.'

'And at present I suppose you'll be found somewhere about that same stile every evening?' said Willoughby foolishly, for he really did not much care whether he met her again or not. Now he was actually in her company, he was surprised at himself for having given her a whole morning's thought; yet the eagerness of her answer flattered him, too.

'Tonight I can't come, worse luck! It's Thursday, and the shops here close of a Thursday at five. I'll havter keep aunt company. But tomorrer? I can be there tomorrer. You'll come, say?'

'Esther!' cried a vexed voice, and the precise, right-minded aunt emerged through a row of raspberry-bushes; 'whatever are you thinking about, delayin' the gentleman in this fashion?' She was full of rustic and official civility for 'the gentleman', but indignant with her niece. 'I don't want none of your London manners down here,' Willoughby heard her say as she marched the girl off.

He himself was not sorry to be released from Esther's too friendly eyes, and he spent an agreeable evening over a book, and this time managed to forget her completely.

Though he remembered her first thing next morning, it was to smile wisely and determine he would not meet her again. Yet by dinner-time the day seemed long; why, after all, should he not meet her? By tea-time prudence triumphed anew—no, he would not go. Then he drank his tea hastily and set off for the stile.

Esther was waiting for him. Expectation had given an additional colour to her cheeks, and her red-brown hair showed here and there a beautiful glint of gold. He could not help admiring the vigorous way in which it waved and twisted, or the little curls which grew at the nape of her neck, tight and close as those of a young lamb's fleece. Her neck here was admirable, too, in its smooth creaminess; and when her eyes lighted up with such evident pleasure at his coming, how avoid the conviction she was a good and nice girl after all?

He proposed they should go down into the little copse on the right, where they would be less disturbed by the occasional passer-by. Here, seated on a felled tree-trunk, Willoughby began that bantering, silly, meaningless form of conversation known among the 'classes' as flirting. He had but the wish to make himself agreeable, and to while away the time. Esther, however, misunderstood him.

Willoughby's hand lay palm downwards on his knee, and she, noticing a ring which he wore on his little finger, took hold of it.

'What a funny ring!' she said; 'let's look?'

To disembarrass himself of her touch, he pulled the ring off and gave it her to examine.

'What's that ugly dark green stone?' she asked.

'It's called a sardonyx.'

'What's it for?' she said, turning it about.

'It's a signet ring, to seal letters with.'

'An' there's a sorter king's head scratched on it, an' some writin' too, only I carnt make it out?'

'It isn't the head of a king, although it wears a crown,' Willoughby explained, 'but the head and bust of a Saracen against whom my ancestor of many hundred years ago went to fight in the Holy Land. And the words cut round it are our motto, "Vertue vauncet", which means virtue prevails.'

Willoughby may have displayed some accession of dignity in giving this bit of family history, for Esther fell into uncontrolled laughter, at which he was much displeased. And when the girl made as though she would put the ring on her own finger, asking, 'Shall I keep it?' he coloured up with sudden annoyance.

'It was only my fun!' said Esther hastily, and gave him the ring back, but his cordiality was gone. He felt no inclination to renew the idle-word pastime, said it was time to go, and, swinging his cane vexedly, struck off the heads of the flowers and the weeds as he went. Esther walked by his side in complete silence, a phenomenon of which he presently became conscious. He felt rather ashamed of having shown temper.

'Well, here's your way home,' said he with an effort at friendliness. 'Goodbye; we've had a nice evening anyhow. It was pleasant down there in the woods, eh?'

He was astonished to see her eyes soften with tears, and to hear the real emotion in her voice as she answered, 'It was just heaven down there with you until you turned so funny-like. What had I done to make you cross? Say you forgive me, do!'

'Silly child!' said Willoughby, completely mollified, 'I'm not the least angry. There, goodbye!' and like a fool he kissed her.

He anathematized his folly in the white light of next morning, and, remembering the kiss he had given her, repented it very sincerely. He had an uncomfortable suspicion she had not received it in the same spirit in which it had been bestowed, but, attaching more serious meaning to it, would build expectations thereon which must be left unfulfilled. It was best indeed not to meet her again; for he acknowledged to himself that, though he only half liked, and even slightly feared her, there was a certain attraction about her—was it in her dark unflinching eyes or in her very red lips?—which might lead him into greater follies still.

Thus it came about that for two successive evenings Esther waited for him in vain, and on the third evening he said to himself, with a grudging relief, that by this time she had probably transferred her affections to someone else.

It was Saturday, the second Saturday since he left town. He spent the day about the farm, contemplated the pigs, inspected the feeding of the stock, and assisted at the afternoon milking. Then at evening, with a refilled pipe, he went for a long lean over the west gate, while he traced fantastic pictures and wove romances in the glories of the sunset clouds.

He watched the colours glow from gold to scarlet, change to crimson, sink at last to sad purple reefs and isles, when the sudden consciousness of someone being near him made him turn round. There stood Esther, and her eyes were full of eagerness and anger.

'Why have you never been to the stile again?' she asked him. 'You promised to come faithful, and you never came. Why have you not kep' your promise? Why? Why?' she persisted, stamping her foot because Willoughby remained silent.

What could he say? Tell her she had no business to follow him like this; or own, what was, unfortunately, the truth, he was just a little glad to see her?

'Praps you don't care for me any more?' she said. 'Well, why did you kiss me, then?'

Why, indeed! thought Willoughby, marvelling at his own idiocy, and yet—such is the inconsistency of man—not wholly without the desire to kiss her again. And while he looked at her she suddenly flung herself down on the hedge-bank at his feet and burst into tears. She did not cover up her face, but simply pressed one cheek down upon the grass while the water poured from her eyes with astonishing abundance. Willoughby saw the dry earth turn dark and moist as it drank the tears in. This, his first experience of Esther's powers of weeping, distressed him horribly; never in his life before had he seen anyone weep like that, he should not have believed such a thing possible; he was alarmed, too, lest she should be noticed from the house. He opened the gate; 'Esther!' he begged, 'don't cry. Come out here, like a dear girl, and let us talk sensibly.'

Because she stumbled, unable to see her way through wet eyes, he gave her his hand, and they found themselves in a field of corn, walking along the narrow grass-path that skirted it, in the shadow of the hedgerow.

'What is there to cry about because you have not seen me for two days?' he began; 'why, Esther, we are only strangers, after all. When we have been at home a week or two we shall scarcely remember each other's names.'

Esther sobbed at intervals, but her tears had ceased. 'It's fine for you to talk of home,' she said to this. 'You've got something that is a home, I s'pose? But me! my home's like hell, with nothing but quarrellin' and cursin', and a father who beats us whether sober or drunk. Yes!' she repeated shrewdly, seeing the lively disgust on Willoughby's face, 'he beat me, all ill as I was, jus' before I come away. I could show you the bruises on my arms still. And now to go back there after knowin' you! It'll be worse than ever. I can't endure it, and I won't! I'll put an end to it or myself somehow, I swear!'

'But my poor Esther, how can I help it? what can I do?' said Willoughby. He was greatly moved, full of wrath with her father, with all the world which makes women suffer. He had suffered himself at the hands of a woman and severely, but this, instead of hardening his heart, had only rendered it the more supple. And yet he had a vivid perception of the peril in which he stood. An interior voice urged him to break away, to seek safety in flight even at the cost of appearing cruel or ridiculous; so, coming to a point in the field where an elm-hole jutted out across the path, he saw with relief he could now withdraw his hand from the girl's, since they must walk singly to skirt round it.

Esther took a step in advance, stopped and suddenly turned to face him; she held out her two hands and her face was very near his own.

'Don't you care for me one little bit?' she said wistfully, and surely sudden madness fell upon him. For he kissed her again, he kissed her many times, he took her in his arms, and pushed all thoughts of the consequences far from him.

But when, an hour later, he and Esther stood by the last gate on the road to Orton, some of these consequences were already calling loudly to him.

'You know I have only £130 a year?' he told her; 'it's no very brilliant prospect for you to marry me on that.'

For he had actually offered her marriage, although to the mediocre man such a proceeding must appear incredible, uncalled for. But to Willoughby, overwhelmed with sadness and remorse, it seemed the only atonement possible.

Sudden exultation leaped at Esther's heart.

'Oh! I'm used to managing' she told him confidently, and mentally resolved to buy herself, so soon as she was married, a black feather boa, such as she had coveted last winter.

Willoughby spent the remaining days of his holiday in thinking out and planning with Esther the details of his return to London and her own, the secrecy to be observed, the necessary legal steps to be taken, and the quiet suburb in which they would set up housekeeping. And, so successfully did he carry out his arrangements, that within five weeks from the day on which he had first met Esther Stables, he and she came out one morning from a church in Highbury, husband and wife. It was a mellow September day, the streets were filled with sunshine, and Willoughby, in reckless high spirits, imagined he saw a reflection of his own gaiety on the indifferent faces of the passersby. There being no one else to perform the office, he congratulated himself very warmly, and Esther's frequent laughter filled in the pauses of the day.

*****

Three months later Willoughby was dining with a friend, and the hour-hand of the clock nearing ten, the host no longer resisted the guest's growing anxiety to be gone. He arose and exchanged with him good wishes and goodbyes.

'Marriage is evidently a most successful institution,' said he, half-jesting, half-sincere; 'you almost make me inclined to go and get married myself. Confess now your thoughts have been at home the whole evening.'

Willoughby thus addressed turned red to the roots of his hair, but did not deny it.

The other laughed. 'And very commendable they should be,' he continued, 'since you are scarcely, so to speak, out of your honeymoon.'

With a social smile on his lips, Willoughby calculated a moment before replying, 'I have been married exactly three months and three days.' Then, after a few words respecting their next meeting, the two shook hands and parted—the young host to finish the evening with books and pipe, the young husband to set out on a twenty minutes' walk to his home.

It was a cold, clear December night following a day of rain. A touch of frost in the air had dried the pavements, and Willoughby's footfall ringing upon the stones re-echoed down the empty suburban street. Above his head was a dark, remote sky thickly powdered with stars, and as he turned westward Alpherat hung for a moment 'comme le point sur un i', over the slender spire of St John's. But he was insensible to the worlds about him; he was absorbed in his own thoughts, and these, as his friend had surmised, were entirely with his wife. For Esther's face was always before his eyes, her voice was always in his ears, she filled the universe for him; yet only four months ago he had never seen her, had never heard her name. This was the curious part of it—here in December he found himself the husband of a girl who was completely dependent upon him not only for food, clothes, and lodging, but for her present happiness, her whole future life; and last July he had been scarcely more than a boy himself, with no greater care on his mind than the pleasant difficulty of deciding where he should spend his annual three weeks' holiday.

But it is events, not months or years, which age. Willoughby, who was only twenty-six, remembered his youth as a sometime companion irrevocably lost to him; its vague, delightful hopes were now crystallized into definite ties, and its happy irresponsibilities displaced by a sense of care, inseparable perhaps from the most fortunate of marriages.

As he reached the street in which he lodged his pace involuntarily slackened. While still some distance off, his eye sought out and distinguished the windows of the room in which Esther awaited him. Through the broken slats of the Venetian blinds he could see the yellow gaslight within. The parlour beneath was in darkness; his landlady had evidently gone to bed, there being no light over the hall-door either. In some apprehension he consulted his watch under the last street-lamp he passed, to find comfort in assuring himself it was only ten minutes after ten. He let himself in with his latch-key, hung up his hat and overcoat by the sense of touch, and, groping his way upstairs, opened the door of the first floor sitting-room.

At the table in the centre of the room sat his wife, leaning upon her elbows, her two hands thrust up into her ruffled hair; spread out before her was a crumpled yesterday's newspaper, and so interested was she to all appearance in its contents that she neither spoke nor looked up as Willoughby entered. Around her were the still uncleared tokens of her last meal: tea-slops, bread-crumbs, and an egg-shell crushed to fragments upon a plate, which was one of those trifles that set Willoughby's teeth on edge—whenever his wife ate an egg she persisted in turning the egg-cup upside down upon the tablecloth, and pounding the shell to pieces in her plate with her spoon.

The room was repulsive in its disorder. The one lighted burner of the gaselier, turned too high, hissed up into a long tongue of flame. The fire smoked feebly under a newly administered shovelful of 'slack', and a heap of ashes and cinders littered the grate. A pair of walking boots, caked in dry mud, lay on the hearth-rug just where they had been thrown off. On the mantelpiece, amidst a dozen other articles which had no business there, was a bedroom-candlestick; and every single article of furniture stood crookedly out of its place.

Willoughby took in the whole intolerable picture, and yet spoke with kindliness. 'Well, Esther! I'm not so late, after all. I hope you did not find the time dull by yourself?' Then he explained the reason of his absence. He had met a friend he had not seen for a couple of years, who had insisted on taking him home to dine.

His wife gave no sign of having heard him; she kept her eyes riveted on the paper before her.

'You received my wire, of course,' Willoughby went on, 'and did not wait?'

Now she crushed the newspaper up with a passionate

movement, and threw it from her. She raised her head, showing cheeks blazing with anger, and dark, sullen, unflinching eyes.

'I did wyte then!' she cried 'I wyted till near eight before I got your old telegraph! I s'pose that's what you call the manners of a "gentleman", to keep your wife mewed up here, while you go gallivantin' off with your fine friends?'

Whenever Esther was angry, which was often, she taunted Willoughby with being 'a gentleman', although this was the precise point about him which at other times found most favour in her eyes. But tonight she was envenomed by the idea he had been enjoying himself without her, stung by fear lest he should have been in company with some other woman.

Willoughby, hearing the taunt, resigned himself to the inevitable. Nothing that he could do might now avert the breaking storm; all his words would only be twisted into fresh griefs. But sad experience had taught him that to take refuge in silence was more fatal still. When Esther was in such a mood as this it was best to supply the fire with fuel, that, through the very violence of the conflagration, it might the sooner burn itself out.

So he said what soothing things he could, and Esther caught them up, disfigured them, and flung them back at him with scorn. She reproached him with no longer caring for her; she vituperated the conduct of his family in never taking the smallest notice of her marriage; and she detailed the insolence of the landlady who had told her that morning she pitied 'poor Mr. Willoughby', and had refused to go out and buy herrings for Esther's early dinner.

Every affront or grievance, real or imaginary, since the day she and

Willoughby had first met, she poured forth with a fluency due to frequent repetition, for, with the exception of today's added injuries,
Willoughby had heard the whole litany many times before.

While she raged and he looked at her, he remembered he had once thought her pretty. He had seen beauty in her rough brown hair, her strong colouring, her full red mouth. He fell into musing ... a woman may lack beauty, he told himself, and yet be loved....

Meanwhile Esther reached white heats of passion, and the strain could no longer be sustained. She broke into sobs and began to shed tears with the facility peculiar to her. In a moment her face was all wet with the big drops which rolled down her cheeks faster and faster, and fell with audible splashes on to the table, on to her lap, on to the floor. To this tearful abundance, formerly a surprising spectacle, Willoughby was now acclimatized; but the remnant of chivalrous feeling not yet extinguished in his bosom forbade him to sit stolidly by while a woman wept, without seeking to console her. As on previous occasions, his peace-overtures were eventually accepted. Esther's tears gradually ceased to flow, she began to exhibit a sort of compunction, she wished to be forgiven, and, with the kiss of reconciliation, passed into a phase of demonstrative affection perhaps more trying to Willoughby's patience than all that had preceded it. 'You don't love me?' she questioned, 'I'm sure you don't love me?' she reiterated; and he asseverated that he loved her until he despised himself. Then at last, only half satisfied, but wearied out with vexation—possibly, too, with a movement of pity at the sight of his haggard face—she consented to leave him. Only, what was he going to do? she asked suspiciously; write those rubbishing stories of his? Well, he must promise not to stay up more than half-an-hour at the latest—only until he had smoked one pipe.

Willoughby promised, as he would have promised anything on earth to secure to himself a half-hour's peace and solitude. Esther groped for her slippers, which were kicked off under the table; scratched four or five matches along the box and threw them away before she succeeded in lighting her candle; set it down again to contemplate her tear-swollen reflection in the chimney-glass, and burst out laughing.

'What a fright I do look, to be sure!' she remarked complacently, and again thrust her two hands up through her disordered curls. Then, holding the candle at such an angle that the grease ran over on to the carpet, she gave Willoughby another vehement kiss and trailed out of the room with an ineffectual attempt to close the door behind her.

Willoughby got up to shut it himself, and wondered why it was that Esther never did any one mortal thing efficiently or well. Good God! how irritable he felt. It was impossible to write. He must find an outlet for his impatience, rend or mend something. He began to straighten the room, but a wave of disgust came over him before the task was fairly commenced. What was the use? Tomorrow all would be bad as before. What was the use of doing anything? He sat down by the table and leaned his head upon his hands.

*****

The past came back to him in pictures: his boyhood's past first of all. He saw again the old home, every inch of which was familiar to him as his own name; he reconstructed in his thought all the old well-known furniture, and replaced it precisely as it had stood long ago. He passed again a childish finger over the rough surface of the faded Utrecht velvet chairs, and smelled again the strong fragrance of the white lilac tree, blowing in through the open parlour-window. He savoured anew the pleasant mental atmosphere produced by the dainty neatness of cultured women, the companionship of a few good pictures, of a few good books. Yet this home had been broken up years ago, the dear familiar things had been scattered far and wide, never to find themselves under the same roof again; and from those near relatives who still remained to him he lived now hopelessly estranged.

Then came the past of his first love-dream, when he worshipped at the feet of Nora Beresford, and, with the whole-heartedness of the true fanatic, clothed his idol with every imaginable attribute of virtue and tenderness. To this day there remained a secret shrine in his heart wherein the Lady of his young ideal was still enthroned, although it was long since he had come to perceive she had nothing whatever in common with the Nora of reality. For the real Nora he had no longer any sentiment, she had passed altogether out of his life and thoughts; and yet, so permanent is all influence, whether good or evil, that the effect she wrought upon his character remained. He recognized tonight that her treatment of him in the past did not count for nothing among the various factors which had determined his fate.

Now, the past of only last year returned, and, strangely enough, this seemed farther removed from him than all the rest. He had been particularly strong, well, and happy this time last year. Nora was dismissed from his mind, and he had thrown all his energies into his work. His tastes were sane and simple, and his dingy, furnished rooms had become through habit very pleasant to him. In being his own, they were invested with a greater charm than another man's castle. Here he had smoked and studied, here he had made many a glorious voyage into the land of books. Many a homecoming, too, rose up before him out of the dark ungenial streets, to a clear blazing fire, a neatly laid cloth, an evening of ideal enjoyment; many a summer twilight when he mused at the open window, plunging his gaze deep into the recesses of his neighbour's lime-tree, where the unseen sparrows chattered with such unflagging gaiety.

He had always been given to much daydreaming, and it was in the silence of his rooms of an evening that he turned his phantasmal adventures into stories for the magazines; here had come to him many an editorial refusal, but here, too, he had received the news of his first unexpected success. All his happiest memories were embalmed in those shabby, badly-furnished rooms.

Now all was changed. Now might there be no longer any soft indulgence of the hour's mood. His rooms and everything he owned belonged now to Esther, too. She had objected to most of his photographs, and had removed them. She hated books, and were he ever so ill-advised as to open one in her presence, she immediately began to talk, no matter how silent or how sullen her previous mood had been. If he read aloud to her she either yawned despairingly, or was tickled into laughter where there was no reasonable cause. At first Willoughby had tried to educate her, and had gone hopefully to the task. It is so natural to think you may make what you will of the woman who loves you. But Esther had no wish to improve. She evinced all the self-satisfaction of an illiterate mind. To her husband's gentle admonitions she replied with brevity that she thought her way quite as good as his; or, if he didn't approve of her pronunciation, he might do the other thing, she was too old to go to school again. He gave up the attempt, and, with humiliation at his previous fatuity, perceived that it was folly to expect that a few weeks of his companionship could alter or pull up the impressions of years, or rather of generations.

Yet here he paused to admit a curious thing: it was not only Esther's bad habits which vexed him, but habits quite unblameworthy in themselves which he never would have noticed in another, irritated him in her. He disliked her manner of standing, of walking, of sitting in a chair, of folding her hands. Like a lover, he was conscious of her proximity without seeing her. Like a lover, too, his eyes followed her every movement, his ear noted every change in her voice. But then, instead of being charmed by everything as the lover is, everything jarred upon him.

What was the meaning of this? Tonight the anomaly pressed upon him: he reviewed his position. Here was he, quite a young man, just twenty-six years of age, married to Esther, and bound to live with her so long as life should last—twenty, forty, perhaps fifty years more. Every day of those years to be spent in her society; he and she face to face, soul to soul; they two alone amid all the whirling, busy, indifferent world. So near together in semblance; in truth, so far apart as regards all that makes life dear.

Willoughby groaned. From the woman he did not love, whom he had never loved, he might not again go free; so much he recognized. The feeling he had once entertained for Esther, strange compound of mistaken chivalry and flattered vanity, was long since extinct; but what, then, was the sentiment with which she inspired him? For he was not indifferent to her—no, never for one instant could he persuade himself he was indifferent, never for one instant could he banish her from his thoughts. His mind's eye followed her during his hours of absence as pertinaciously as his bodily eye dwelt upon her actual presence. She was the principal object of the universe to him, the centre around which his wheel of life revolved with an appalling fidelity.

What did it mean? What could it mean? he asked himself with anguish.

And the sweat broke out upon his forehead and his hands grew cold, for on a sudden the truth lay there like a written word upon the tablecloth before him. This woman, whom he had taken to himself for better, for worse, inspired him with a passion, intense indeed, all-masterful, soul-subduing as Love itself.... But when he understood the terror of his Hatred, he laid his head upon his arms and wept, not facile tears like Esther's, but tears wrung out from his agonizing, unavailing regret.

'A POOR STICK'
By Arthur Morrison

(Tales of Mean Streets, London: Methuen and Co., 1894) Published by permission of Methuen and Co.

Mrs. Jennings (or Jinnins, as the neighbours would have it) ruled absolutely at home, when she took so much trouble as to do anything at all there—which was less often than might have been. As for Robert her husband, he was a poor stick, said the neighbours. And yet he was a man with enough of hardihood to remain a non-unionist in the erectors' shop at Maidment's all the years of his service; no mean test of a man's fortitude and resolution, as many a sufferer for independent opinion might testify. The truth was that Bob never grew out of his courtship-blindness. Mrs. Jennings governed as she pleased, stayed out or came home as she chose, and cooked a dinner or didn't, as her inclination stood. Thus it was for ten years, during which time there were no children, and Bob bore all things uncomplaining: cooking his own dinner when he found none cooked, and sewing on his own buttons. Then of a sudden came children, till in three years there were three; and Bob Jennings had to nurse and to wash them as often as not.

Mrs. Jennings at this time was what is called rather a fine woman: a woman of large scale and full development; whose slatternly habit left her coarse black hair to tumble in snake-locks about her face and shoulders half the day; who, clad in half-hooked clothes, bore herself notoriously and unabashed in her fullness; and of whom ill things were said regarding the lodger. The gossips had their excuse. The lodger was an irregular young cabinet-maker, who lost quarters and halves and whole days;

who had been seen abroad with his landlady, what time Bob Jennings was putting the children to bed at home; who on his frequent holidays brought in much beer, which he and the woman shared, while Bob was at work. To carry the tale to Bob would have been a thankless errand, for he would have none of anybody's sympathy, even in regard to miseries plain to his eye. But the thing got about in the workshop, and there his days were made bitter.

At home things grew worse. To return at half-past five, and find the children still undressed, screaming, hungry and dirty, was a matter of habit: to get them food, to wash them, to tend the cuts and bumps sustained through the day of neglect, before lighting a fire and getting tea for himself, were matters of daily duty. 'Ah,' he said to his sister, who came at intervals to say plain things about Mrs. Jennings, 'you shouldn't go for to set a man agin 'is wife, Jin. Melier do'n' like work, I know, but that's nach'ral to 'er. She ought to married a swell 'stead o' me; she might 'a' done easy if she liked, bein' sich a fine gal; but she's good-'arted, is Melier; an' she can't 'elp bein' a bit thoughtless.' Whereat his sister called him a fool (it was her customary goodbye at such times), and took herself off.

Bob Jennings's intelligence was sufficient for his common needs, but it was never a vast intelligence. Now, under a daily burden of dull misery, it clouded and stooped. The base wit of the workshop he comprehended less, and realized more slowly, than before; and the gaffer cursed him for a sleepy dolt.

Mrs. Jennings ceased from any pretence of housewifery, and would sometimes sit—perchance not quite sober—while Bob washed the children in the evening, opening her mouth only to express her contempt for him and his establishment, and to make him understand that she was sick of both. Once, exasperated by his quietness, she struck at him, and for a moment he was another man. 'Don't do that, Melier,' he said, 'else I might forget myself.' His manner surprised his wife: and it was such that she never did do that again.

So was Bob Jennings: without a friend in the world, except his sister, who chid him, and the children, who squalled at him: when his wife vanished with the lodger, the clock, a shade of wax flowers, Bob's best boots (which fitted the lodger), and his silver watch. Bob had returned, as usual, to the dirt and the children, and it was only when he struck a light that he found the clock was gone.

'Mummy tooked ve t'ock,' said Milly, the eldest child, who had followed him in from the door, and now gravely observed his movements. 'She tooked ve t'ock an' went ta-ta. An' she tooked ve fyowers.'

Bob lit the paraffin lamp with the green glass reservoir, and carried it and its evil smell about the house. Some things had been turned over and others had gone, plainly. All Melier's clothes were gone. The lodger was not in, and under his bedroom window, where his box had stood, there was naught but an oblong patch of conspicuously clean wallpaper. In a muddle of doubt and perplexity, Bob found himself at the front door, staring up and down the street. Divers women-neighbours stood at their doors, and eyed him curiously; for Mrs. Webster, moralist, opposite, had not watched the day's proceedings (nor those of many other days) for nothing, nor had she kept her story to herself.

He turned back into the house, a vague notion of what had befallen percolating feebly through his bewilderment. 'I dunno—I dunno,' he faltered, rubbing his ear. His mouth was dry, and he moved his lips uneasily, as he gazed with aimless looks about the walls and ceiling. Presently his eyes rested on the child, and 'Milly,' he said decisively, 'come an 'ave yer face washed.'

He put the children to bed early, and went out. In the morning, when his sister came, because she had heard the news in common with everybody else, he had not returned. Bob Jennings had never lost more than two quarters in his life, but he was not seen at the workshop all this day. His sister stayed in the house, and in the evening, at his regular homing-time, he appeared, haggard and dusty, and began his preparations for washing the children. When he was made to understand that they had been already attended to, he looked doubtful and troubled for a moment. Presently he said: 'I ain't found 'er yet, Jin; I was in 'opes she might 'a' bin back by this. I—I don't expect she'll be very long. She was alwis a bit larky, was Melier; but very good-'arted.'

His sister had prepared a strenuous lecture on the theme of 'I told you so'; but the man was so broken, so meek, and so plainly unhinged in his faculties, that she suppressed it. Instead, she gave him comfortable talk, and made him promise in the end to sleep that night, and take up his customary work in the morning.

He did these things, and could have worked placidly enough had he but been alone; but the tale had reached the workshop, and there was no lack of brutish chaff to disorder him. This the decenter men would have no part in, and even protested against. But the ill-conditioned kept their way, till, at the cry of 'Bell O!' when all were starting for dinner, one of the worst shouted the cruellest gibe of all. Bob Jennings turned on him and knocked him over a scrap-heap.

A shout went up from the hurrying workmen, with a chorus of 'Serve ye right,' and the fallen joker found himself awkwardly confronted by the shop bruiser. But Bob had turned to a corner, and buried his eyes in the bend of his arm, while his shoulders heaved and shook.

He slunk away home, and stayed there: walking restlessly to and fro, and often peeping down the street from the window. When, at twilight, his sister came again, he had become almost cheerful, and said with some briskness: 'I'm agoin' to meet 'er, Jin, at seven. I know where she'll be waitin'.'

He went upstairs, and after a little while came down again in his best black coat, carefully smoothing a tall hat of obsolete shape with his pocket-handkerchief. 'I ain't wore it for years,' he said. 'I ought to 'a' wore it—it might 'a' pleased 'er. She used to say she wouldn't walk with me in no other—when I used to meet 'er in the evenin', at seven o'clock.' He brushed assiduously, and put the hat on. 'I'd better 'ave a shave round the corner as I go along,' he added, fingering his stubbly chin.

He received as one not comprehending his sister's persuasion to remain at home; but when he went she followed at a little distance. After his penny shave he made for the main road, where company-keeping couples walked up and down all evening. He stopped at a church, and began pacing slowly to and fro before it, eagerly looking out each way as he went.

His sister watched him for nearly half an hour, and then went home. In two hours more she came back with her husband. Bob was still there, walking to and fro.

''Ullo, Bob,' said his brother-in-law; 'come along 'ome an' get to bed, there's a good chap. You'll be awright in the mornin'.'

'She ain't turned up,' Bob complained, 'or else I've missed 'er. This is the reg'lar place—where I alwis used to meet 'er. But she'll come tomorrer. She used to leave me in the lurch sometimes, bein' nach'rally larky. But very good-'arted, mindjer; very good-'arted.'

She did not come the next evening, nor the next, nor the evening after, nor the one after that. But Bob Jennings, howbeit depressed and anxious, was always confident. 'Somethink's prevented 'er tonight,' he would say, 'but she'll come tomorrer.... I'll buy a blue tie tomorrer—she used to like me in a blue tie. I won't miss 'er tomorrer. I'll come a little earlier.'

So it went. The black coat grew ragged in the service, and hobbledehoys, finding him safe sport, smashed the tall hat over his eyes time after time. He wept over the hat, and straightened it as best he might. Was she coming? Night after night, and night and night. But tomorrow....

THE ADVENTURE OF THE ABBEY GRANGE
By Arthur Conan Doyle

(The Strand Magazine, 23 January 1897)

It was on a bitterly cold night and frosty morning, towards the end of the winter of '97, that I was awakened by a tugging at my shoulder. It was Holmes. The candle in his hand shone upon his eager, stooping face, and told me at a glance that something was amiss.

'Come, Watson, come!' he cried. The game is afoot. Not a word! Into your clothes and come!'

Ten minutes later we were both in a cab, and rattling through the silent streets on our way to Charing Cross Station. The first faint winter's dawn was beginning to appear, and we could dimly see the occasional figure of an early workman as he passed us, blurred and indistinct in the opalescent London reek. Holmes nestled in silence into his heavy coat, and I was glad to do the same, for the air was most bitter, and neither of us had broken our fast.

It was not until we had consumed some hot tea at the station and taken our places in the Kentish train that we were sufficiently thawed, he to speak and I to listen. Holmes drew a note from his pocket, and read aloud:

Abbey Grange, Marsham, Kent
3:30 A.M.

My Dear Mr. Holmes:

I should be very glad of your immediate assistance in what promises to be a most remarkable case. It is something quite in your line. Except for releasing the lady I will see that everything is kept exactly as I have found it, but I beg you not to lose an instant, as it is difficult to leave Sir Eustace there.

Yours faithfully,
STANLEY HOPKINS

'Hopkins has called me in seven times, and on each occasion his summons has been entirely justified,' said Holmes. 'I fancy that every one of his cases has found its way into your collection, and I must admit, Watson, that you have some power of selection, which atones for much which I deplore in your narratives. Your fatal habit of looking at everything from the point of view of a story instead of as a scientific exercise has ruined what might have been an instructive and even classical series of demonstrations. You slur over work of the utmost finesse and delicacy, in order to dwell upon sensational details which may excite, but cannot possibly instruct, the reader.'

'Why do you not write them yourself?' I said, with some bitterness.

'I will, my dear Watson, I will. At present I am, as you know, fairly busy, but I propose to devote my declining years to the composition of a textbook, which shall focus the whole art of detection into one volume. Our present research appears to be a case of murder.'

'You think this Sir Eustace is dead, then?'

'I should say so. Hopkins's writing shows considerable agitation, and he is not an emotional man. Yes, I gather there has been violence, and that the body is left for our inspection. A mere suicide would not have caused him to send for me. As to the release of the lady, it would appear that she has been locked in her room during the tragedy. We are moving in high life, Watson, crackling paper, 'E.B.' monogram, coat-of-arms, picturesque address. I think that friend Hopkins will live up to his reputation, and that we shall have an interesting morning. The crime was committed before twelve last night.'

'How can you possibly tell?'

'By an inspection of the trains, and by reckoning the time. The local police had to be called in, they had to communicate with Scotland Yard, Hopkins had to go out, and he in turn had to send for me. All that makes a fair night's work. Well, here we are at Chislehurst Station, and we shall soon set our doubts at rest.'

A drive of a couple of miles through narrow country lanes brought us to a park gate, which was opened for us by an old lodge-keeper, whose haggard face bore the reflection of some great disaster. The avenue ran through a noble park, between lines of ancient elms, and ended in a low, widespread house, pillared in front after the fashion of Palladio. The central part was evidently of a great age and shrouded in ivy, but the large windows showed that modern changes had been carried out, and one wing of the house appeared to be entirely new. The youthful figure and alert, eager face of Inspector Stanley Hopkins confronted us in the open doorway.

'I'm very glad you have come, Mr. Holmes. And you, too, Dr. Watson. But, indeed, if I had my time over again, I should not have troubled you, for since the lady has come to herself, she has given so clear an account of the affair that there is not much left for us to do. You remember that Lewisham gang of burglars?'

'What, the three Randalls?'

'Exactly; the father and two sons. It's their work. I have not a doubt of it. They did a job at Sydenham a fortnight ago and were seen and described. Rather cool to do another so soon and so near, but it is they, beyond all doubt. It's a hanging matter this time.'

'Sir Eustace is dead, then?'

'Yes, his head was knocked in with his own poker.'

'Sir Eustace Brackenstall, the driver tells me.'

'Exactly—one of the richest men in Kent—Lady Brackenstall is in the morning-room. Poor lady, she has had a most dreadful experience. She seemed half dead when I saw her first. I think you had best see her and hear her account of the facts. Then we will examine the dining-room together.'

Lady Brackenstall was no ordinary person. Seldom have I seen so graceful a figure, so womanly a presence, and so beautiful a face. She was a blonde, golden-haired, blue-eyed, and would no doubt have had the perfect complexion which goes with such colouring, had not her recent experience left her drawn and haggard. Her sufferings were physical as well as mental, for over one eye rose a hideous, plum-coloured swelling, which her maid, a tall, austere woman, was bathing assiduously with vinegar and water. The lady lay back exhausted upon a couch, but her quick, observant gaze, as we entered the room, and the alert expression of her beautiful features, showed that neither her wits nor her courage had been shaken by her terrible experience. She was enveloped in a loose dressing-gown of blue and silver, but a black sequin-covered dinner-dress lay upon the couch beside her.

'I have told you all that happened, Mr. Hopkins,' she said,

wearily. 'Could you not repeat it for me? Well, if you think it necessary, I will tell these gentlemen what occurred. Have they been in the dining-room yet?'

'I thought they had better hear your ladyship's story first.'

'I shall be glad when you can arrange matters. It is horrible to me to think of him still lying there.' She shuddered and buried her face in her hands. As she did so, the loose gown fell back from her forearms. Holmes uttered an exclamation.

'You have other injuries, madam! What is this?' Two vivid red spots stood out on one of the white, round limbs. She hastily covered it.

'It is nothing. It has no connection with this hideous business tonight.
If you and your friend will sit down, I will tell you all I can.

'I am the wife of Sir Eustace Brackenstall. I have been married about a year. I suppose that it is no use my attempting to conceal that our marriage has not been a happy one. I fear that all our neighbours would tell you that, even if I were to attempt to deny it. Perhaps the fault may be partly mine. I was brought up in the freer, less conventional atmosphere of South Australia, and this English life, with its proprieties and its primness, is not congenial to me. But the main reason lies in the one fact, which is notorious to everyone, and that is that Sir Eustace was a confirmed drunkard. To be with such a man for an hour is unpleasant. Can you imagine what it means for a sensitive and high-spirited woman to be tied to him for day and night? It is a sacrilege, a crime, a villany to hold that such a marriage is binding. I say that these monstrous laws of yours will bring a curse upon the land—God will not let such wickedness endure.' For an instant she sat up, her cheeks flushed, and her eyes blazing from under the terrible mark upon her brow. Then the strong, soothing hand of the austere maid drew her head down on to the cushion, and the wild anger died away into passionate sobbing. At last she continued:

'I will tell you about last night. You are aware, perhaps, that in this house all the servants sleep in the modern wing. This central block is made up of the dwelling-rooms, with the kitchen behind and our bedroom above. My maid, Theresa, sleeps above my room. There is no one else, and no sound could alarm those who are in the farther wing. This must have been well known to the robbers, or they would not have acted as they did.

'Sir Eustace retired about half-past ten. The servants had already gone to their quarters. Only my maid was up, and she had remained in her room at the top of the house until I needed her services. I sat until after eleven in this room, absorbed in a book. Then I walked round to see that all was right before I went upstairs. It was my custom to do this myself, for, as I have explained, Sir Eustace was not always to be trusted. I went into the kitchen, the butler's pantry, the gun-room, the billiard-room, the drawing-room, and finally the dining-room. As I approached the window, which is covered with thick curtains, I suddenly felt the wind blow upon my face and realized that it was open. I flung the curtain aside and found myself face to face with a broad shouldered elderly man, who had just stepped into the room. The window is a long French one, which really forms a door leading to the lawn. I held my bedroom candle lit in my hand, and, by its light, behind the first man I saw two others, who were in the act of entering. I stepped back, but the fellow was on me in an instant. He caught me first by the wrist and then by the throat. I opened my mouth to scream, but he struck me a savage blow with his fist over the eye, and felled me to the ground. I must have been unconscious for a few minutes, for when I came to myself, I found that they had torn down the bell-rope, and had secured me tightly to the oaken chair which stands at the head of the dining-table. I was so firmly bound that I could not move, and a handkerchief round my mouth prevented me from uttering a sound. It was at this instant that my unfortunate husband entered the room. He had evidently heard some suspicious sounds, and he came prepared for such a scene as he found. He was dressed in nightshirt and trousers, with his favourite blackthorn cudgel in his hand. He rushed at the burglars, but another—it was an elderly man—stooped, picked the poker out of the grate and struck him a horrible blow as he passed. He fell with a groan and never moved again. I fainted once more, but again it could only have been for a very few minutes during which I was insensible. When I opened my eyes I found that they had collected the silver from the sideboard, and they had drawn a bottle of wine which stood there. Each of them had a glass in his hand. I have already told you, have I not, that one was elderly, with a beard, and the others young, hairless lads. They might have been a father and his two sons. They talked together in whispers. Then they came over and made sure that I was securely bound. Finally they withdrew, closing the window after them. It was quite a quarter of an hour before I got my mouth free. When I did so, my screams brought the maid to my assistance. The other servants were soon alarmed, and we sent for the local police, who instantly communicated with London. That is really all that I can tell you, gentlemen, and I trust that it will not be necessary for me to go over so painful a story again.'

'Any questions, Mr. Holmes?' asked Hopkins.

'I will not impose any further tax upon Lady Brackenstall's patience and time,' said Holmes. 'Before I go into the dining-room, I should like to hear your experience.' He looked at the maid.

'I saw the men before ever they came into the house,' said she. 'As I sat by my bedroom window I saw three men in the moonlight down by the lodge gate yonder, but I thought nothing of it at the time. It was more than an hour after that I heard my mistress scream, and down I ran, to find her, poor lamb, just as she says, and him on the floor, with his blood and brains over the room. It was enough to drive a woman out of her wits, tied there, and her very dress spotted with him, but she never wanted courage, did Miss Mary Fraser of Adelaide and Lady Brackenstall of Abbey Grange hasn't learned new ways. You've questioned her long enough, you gentlemen, and now she is coming to her own room, just with her old Theresa, to get the rest that she badly needs.'

With a motherly tenderness the gaunt woman put her arm round her mistress and led her from the room.

'She had been with her all her life,' said Hopkins. 'Nursed her as a baby, and came with her to England when they first left Australia, eighteen months ago. Theresa Wright is her name, and the kind of maid you don't pick up nowadays. This way, Mr. Holmes, if you please!'

The keen interest had passed out of Holmes's expressive face, and I knew that with the mystery all the charm of the case had departed. There still remained an arrest to be effected, but what were these commonplace rogues that he should soil his hands with them? An abstruse and learned specialist who finds that he has been called in for a case of measles would experience something of the annoyance which I read in my friend's eyes. Yet the scene in the dining-room of the Abbey Grange was sufficiently strange to arrest his attention and to recall his waning interest.

It was a very large and high chamber, with carved oak ceiling, oaken panelling, and a fine array of deer's heads and ancient weapons around the walls. At the further end from the door was the high French window of which we had heard. Three smaller windows on the right-hand side filled the apartment with cold winter sunshine. On the left was a large, deep fireplace, with a massive, overhanging oak mantelpiece. Beside the fireplace was a heavy oaken chair with arms and crossbars at the bottom. In and out through the open woodwork was woven a crimson cord, which was secured at each side to the crosspiece below. In releasing the lady, the cord had been slipped off her, but the knots with which it had been secured still remained. These details only struck our attention afterwards, for our thoughts were entirely absorbed by the terrible object which lay upon the tiger-skin heathrug in front of the fire.

It was the body of a tall, well-made man, about forty years of age. He lay upon his back, his face upturned, with his white teeth grinning through his short, black beard. His two clenched hands were raised above his head, and a heavy, blackthorn stick lay across them. His dark, handsome, aquiline features were convulsed into a spasm of vindictive hatred, which had set his dead face in a terribly fiendish expression. He had evidently been in his bed when the alarm had broken out, for he wore a foppish, embroidered nightshirt, and his bare feet projected from his trousers. His head was horribly injured, and the whole room bore witness to the savage ferocity of the blow which had struck him down. Beside him lay the heavy poker, bent into a curve by the concussion. Holmes examined both it and the indescribable wreck which it had wrought.

'He must be a powerful man, this elder Randall,' he remarked.

'Yes,' said Hopkins. 'I have some record of the fellow, and he is a rough customer.'

'You should have no difficulty in getting him.'

'Not the slightest. We have been on the look-out for him, and there was some idea that he had got away to America. Now that we know that the gang are here, I don't see how they can escape. We have the news at every seaport already, and a reward will be offered before evening. What beats me is how they could have done so mad a thing, knowing that the lady could describe them and that we could not fail to recognize the description.'

'Exactly. One would have expected that they would silence Lady Brackenstall as well.'

'They may not have realized,' I suggested, 'that she had recovered from her faint.'

'That is likely enough. If she seemed to be senseless, they would not take her life. What about this poor fellow, Hopkins? I seem to have heard some queer stories about him.'

'He was a good-hearted man when he was sober, but a perfect fiend when he was drunk, or rather when he was half drunk, for he seldom really went the whole way. The devil seemed to be in him at such times, and he was capable of anything. From what I hear, in spite of all his wealth and his title, he very nearly came our way once or twice. There was a scandal about his drenching a dog with petroleum and setting it on fire—her ladyship's dog, to make the matter worse—and that was only hushed up with difficulty. Then he threw a decanter at that maid, Theresa Wright—there was trouble about that. On the whole, and between ourselves, it will be a brighter house without him. What are you looking at now?'

Holmes was down on his knees, examining with great attention the knots upon the red cord with which the lady had been secured. Then he carefully scrutinized the broken and frayed end where it had snapped off when the burglar had dragged it down.

'When this was pulled down, the bell in the kitchen must have rung loudly,' he remarked.

'No one could hear it. The kitchen stands right at the back of the house.'

'How did the burglar know no one would hear it? How dared he pull at a bell-rope in that reckless fashion?'

'Exactly, Mr. Holmes, exactly. You put the very question which I have asked myself again and again. There can be no doubt that this fellow must have known the house and its habits. He must have perfectly understood that the servants would all be in bed at that comparatively early hour, and that no one could possibly hear a bell ring in the kitchen. Therefore, he must have been in close league with one of the servants. Surely that is evident. But there are eight servants, and all of good character.'

'Other things being equal,' said Holmes, 'one would suspect the one at whose head the master threw a decanter. And yet that would involve treachery towards the mistress to whom this woman seems devoted. Well, well, the point is a minor one, and when you have Randall you will probably find no difficulty in securing his accomplice. The lady's story certainly seems to be corroborated, if it needed corroboration, by every detail which we see before us.' He walked to the French window and threw it open. 'There are no signs here, but the ground is iron hard, and one would not expect them. I see that these candles in the mantelpiece have been lighted.'

'Yes, it was by their light, and that of the lady's bedroom candle, that the burglars saw their way about.'

'And what did they take?'

'Well, they did not take much—only half a dozen articles of plate off the sideboard. Lady Brackenstall thinks that they were themselves so disturbed by the death of Sir Eustace that they did not ransack the house, as they would otherwise have done.'

'No doubt that is true, and yet they drank some wine, I understand.'

To steady their nerves.'

'Exactly. These three glasses upon the sideboard have been untouched, I suppose?'

'Yes, and the bottle stands as they left it.'

'Let us look at it. Halloa, halloa! What is this?'

The three glasses were grouped together, all of them tinged with wine, and one of them containing some dregs of beeswing. The bottle stood near them, two-thirds full, and beside it lay a long, deeply stained cork. Its appearance and the dust upon the bottle showed that it was no common vintage which the murderers had enjoyed.

A change had come over Holmes's manner. He had lost his listless expression, and again I saw an alert light of interest in his keen, deepset eyes. He raised the cork and examined it minutely.

'How did they draw it?' he asked.

Hopkins pointed to a half-opened drawer. In it lay some table linen and a large corkscrew.

'Did Lady Brackenstall say that screw was used?'

'No, you remember that she was senseless at the moment when the bottle was opened.'

'Quite so. As a matter of fact, that screw was not used. This bottle was opened by a pocket screw, probably contained in a knife, and not more than an inch and a half long. If you will examine the top of the cork, you will observe that the screw was driven in three times before the cork was extracted. It has never been transfixed. This long screw would have transfixed it and drawn it up with a single pull. When you catch this fellow, you will find that he has one of these multiplex knives in his possession.'

'Excellent!' said Hopkins.

'But these glasses do puzzle me, I confess. Lady Brackenstall actually saw the three men drinking, did she not?'

'Yes; she was clear about that.'

'Then there is an end of it. What more is to be said? And yet, you must admit, that the three glasses are very remarkable, Hopkins. What? You see nothing remarkable? Well, well, let it pass. Perhaps, when a man has special knowledge and special powers like my own, it rather encourages him to seek a complex explanation when a simpler one is at hand. Of course, it must be a mere chance about the glasses. Well, good-morning, Hopkins. I don't see that I can be of any use to you, and you appear to have your case very clear. You will let me know when Randall is arrested, and any further developments which may occur. I trust that I shall soon have to congratulate you upon a successful conclusion. Come, Watson, I fancy that we may employ ourselves more profitably at home.'

During our return journey, I could see by Holmes's face that he was much puzzled by something which he had observed. Every now and then, by an effort, he would throw off the impression, and talk as if the matter were clear, but then his doubts would settle down upon him again, and his knitted brows and abstracted eyes would show that his thoughts had gone back once more to the great dining-room of the Abbey Grange, in which this midnight tragedy had been enacted. At last, by a sudden impulse, just as our train was crawling out of a suburban station, he sprang on to the platform and pulled me out after him.

'Excuse me, my dear fellow,' said he, as we watched the rear carriages of our train disappearing round a curve, 'I am sorry to make you the victim of what may seem a mere whim, but on my life, Watson, I simply can't leave that case in this condition. Every instinct that I possess cries out against it. It's wrong—it's all wrong—I'll swear that it's wrong. And yet the lady's story was complete, the maid's corroboration was sufficient, the detail was fairly exact. What have I to put up against that? Three wineglasses, that is all. But if I had not taken things for granted, if I had examined everything with care which I should have shown had we approached the case de novo and had no cut-and-dried story to warp my mind, should I not then have found something more definite to go upon? Of course I should. Sit down on this bench, Watson, until a train for Chislehurst arrives, and allow me to lay the evidence before you, imploring you in the first instance to dismiss from your mind the idea that anything which the maid or her mistress may have said must necessarily be true. The lady's charming personality must not be permitted to warp our judgment.

'Surely there are details in her story which, if we looked at in cold blood, would excite our suspicion. These burglars made a considerable haul at Sydenham a fortnight ago. Some account of them and of their appearance was in the papers, and would naturally occur to anyone who wished to invent a story in which imaginary robbers should play a part. As a matter of fact, burglars who have done a good stroke of business are, as a rule, only too glad to enjoy the proceeds in peace and quiet without embarking on another perilous undertaking. Again, it is unusual for burglars to operate at so early an hour, it is unusual for burglars to strike a lady to prevent her screaming, since one would imagine that was the sure way to make her scream, it is unusual for them to commit murder when their numbers are sufficient to overpower one man, it is unusual for them to be content with a limited plunder when there was much more within their reach, and finally, I should say, that it was very unusual for such men to leave a bottle half empty. How do all these unusuals strike you, Watson?'

'Their cumulative effect is certainly considerable, and yet each of them is quite possible in itself. The most unusual thing of all, as it seems to me, is that the lady should be tied to the chair.'

'Well, I am not so clear about that, Watson, for it is evident that they must either kill her or else secure her in such a way that she could not give immediate notice of their escape. But at any rate I have shown, have I not, that there is a certain element of improbability about the lady's story? And now, on the top of this, comes the incident of the wineglasses.'

'What about the wineglasses?'

'Can you see them in your mind's eye?'

'I see them clearly.'

'We are told that three men drank from them. Does that strike you as likely?'

'Why not? There was wine in each glass.'

'Exactly, but there was beeswing only in one glass. You must have noticed that fact. What does that suggest to your mind?'

'The last glass filled would be most likely to contain beeswing.'

'Not at all. The bottle was full of it, and it is inconceivable that the first two glasses were clear and the third heavily charged with it. There are two possible explanations, and only two. One is that after the second glass was filled the bottle was violently agitated, and so the third glass received the beeswing. That does not appear probable. No, no, I am sure that I am right.'

'What, then, do you suppose?'

'That only two glasses were used, and that the dregs of both were poured into a third glass, so as to give the false impression that three people had been here. In that way all the beeswing would be in the last glass, would it not? Yes, I am convinced that this is so. But if I have hit upon the true explanation of this one small phenomenon, then in an instant the case rises from the commonplace to the exceedingly remarkable, for it can only mean that Lady Brackenstall and her maid have deliberately lied to us, that not one word of their story is to be believed, that they have some very strong reason for covering the real criminal, and that we must construct our case for ourselves without any help from them. That is the mission which now lies before us, and here, Watson, is the Sydenham train.'

The household at the Abbey Grange were much surprised at our return, but Sherlock Holmes, finding that Stanley Hopkins had gone off to report to headquarters, took possession of the dining-room, locked the door upon the inside, and devoted himself for two hours to one of those minute and laborious investigations which form the solid basis on which his brilliant edifices of deduction were reared. Seated in a corner like an interested student who observes the demonstration of his professor, I followed every step of that remarkable research. The window, the curtains, the carpet, the chair, the rope—each in turn was minutely examined and duly pondered. The body of the unfortunate baronet had been removed, and all else remained as we had seen it in the morning. Finally, to my astonishment, Holmes climbed up on to the massive mantelpiece. Far above his head hung the few inches of red cord which were still attached to the wire. For a long time he gazed upward at it, and then in an attempt to get nearer to it he rested his knee upon a wooden bracket on the wall. This brought his hand within a few inches of the broken end of the rope, but it was not this so much as the bracket itself which seemed to engage his attention. Finally, he sprang down with an ejaculation of satisfaction.

'It's all right, Watson,' said he. 'We have got our case—one of the most remarkable in our collection. But, dear me, how slow-witted I have been, and how nearly I have committed the blunder of my lifetime! Now, I think that, with a few missing links, my chain is almost complete.'

'You have got your men?'

'Man, Watson, man. Only one, but a very formidable person. Strong as a lion—witness the blow that bent that poker! Six foot three in height, active as a squirrel, dexterous with his fingers, finally, remarkably quick-witted, for this whole ingenious story is of his concoction. Yes, Watson, we have come upon the handiwork of a very remarkable individual. And yet, in that bell-rope, he has given us a clue which should not have left us a doubt.'

'Where was the clue?'

'Well, if you were to pull down a bell-rope, Watson, where would you expect it to break? Surely at the spot where it is attached to the wire. Why should it break three inches from the top, as this one has done?'

'Because it is frayed there?'

'Exactly. This end, which we can examine, is frayed. He was cunning enough to do that with his knife. But the other end is not frayed. You could not observe that from here, but if you were on the mantelpiece you would see that it is cut clean off without any mark of fraying whatever. You can reconstruct what occurred. The man needed the rope. He would not tear it down for fear of giving the alarm by ringing the bell. What did he do? He sprang up on the mantelpiece, could not quite reach it, put his knee on the bracket—you will see the impression in the dust—and so got his knife to bear upon the cord. I could not reach the place by at least three inches—from which I infer that he is at least three inches a bigger man than I. Look at that mark upon the seat of the oaken chair! What is it?'

'Blood.'

'Undoubtedly it is blood. This alone puts the lady's story out of court. If she were seated on the chair when the crime was done, how comes that mark? No, no, she was placed in the chair after the death of her husband. I'll wager that the black dress shows a corresponding mark to this. We have not yet met our Waterloo, Watson, but this is our Marengo, for it begins in defeat and ends in victory. I should like now to have a few words with the nurse,

Theresa. We must be wary for a while, if we are to get the information which we want.'

She was an interesting person, this stern Australian nurse—taciturn, suspicious, ungracious, it took some time before Holmes's pleasant manner and frank acceptance of all that she said thawed her into a corresponding amiability. She did not attempt to conceal her hatred for her late employer.

'Yes, sir, it is true that he threw the decanter at me. I heard him call my mistress a name, and I told him that he would not dare to speak so if her brother had been there. Then it was that he threw it at me. He might have thrown a dozen if he had but left my bonny bird alone. He was forever ill-treating her, and she too proud to complain. She will not even tell me all that he has done to her. She never told me of those marks on her arm that you saw this morning, but I know very well that they come from a stab with a hatpin. The sly devil—God forgive me that I should speak of him so, now that he is dead! But a devil he was, if ever one walked the earth. He was all honey when first we met him—only eighteen months ago, and we both feel as if it were eighteen years. She had only just arrived in London. Yes, it was her first voyage—she had never been from home before. He won her with his title and his money and his false London ways. If she made a mistake she has paid for it, if ever a woman did. What month did we meet him? Well, I tell you it was just after we arrived. We arrived in June, and it was July. They were married in January of last year. Yes, she is down in the morning-room again, and I have no doubt she will see you, but you must not ask too much of her, for she has gone through all that flesh and blood will stand.'

Lady Brackenstall was reclining on the same couch, but looked brighter than before. The maid had entered with us, and began once more to foment the bruise upon her mistress's brow.

'I hope,' said the lady, 'that you have not come to cross-examine me again?'

'No,' Holmes answered, in his gentlest voice. 'I will not cause you any unnecessary trouble, Lady Brackenstall, and my whole desire is to make things easy for you, for I am convinced that you are a much-tried woman. If you will treat me as a friend and trust me, you may find that I will justify your trust.'

'What do you want me to do?'

'To tell me the truth.'

'Mr. Holmes!'

'No, no, Lady Brackenstall—it is no use. You may have heard of any little reputation which I possess. I will stake it all on the fact that your story is an absolute fabrication.'

Mistress and maid were both staring at Holmes with pale faces and frightened eyes.

'You are an impudent fellow!' cried Theresa. 'Do you mean to say that my mistress has told a lie?'

Holmes rose from his chair.

'Have you nothing to tell me?'

'I have told you everything.'

'Think once more, Lady Brackenstall. Would it not be better to be frank?'

For an instant there was hesitation in her beautiful face. Then some new strong thought caused it to set like a mask.

'I have told you all I know.'

Holmes took his hat and shrugged his shoulders. 'I am sorry,' he said, and without another word we left the room and the house. There was a pond in the park, and to this my friend led the way. It was frozen over, but a single hole was left for the convenience of a solitary swan. Holmes gazed at it, and then passed on to the lodge gate. There he scribbled a short note for Stanley Hopkins, and left it with the lodge-keeper.

'It may be a hit, or it may be a miss, but we are bound to do something for friend Hopkins, just to justify this second visit,' said he. 'I will not quite take him into my confidence yet. I think our next scene of operations must be the shipping office of the Adelaide-Southampton line, which stands at the end of Pall Mall, if I remember right. There is a second line of steamers which connect South Australia with England, but we will draw the larger cover first.'

Holmes's card sent in to the manager ensured instant attention, and he was not long in acquiring all the information he needed. In June of '95, only one of their line had reached a home port. It was the Rock of Gibraltar, their largest and best boat. A reference to the passenger list showed that Miss Fraser, of Adelaide, with her maid had made the voyage in her. The boat was now somewhere south of the Suez Canal on her way to Australia. Her officers were the same as in '95, with one exception. The first officer, Mr. Jack Crocker, had been made a captain and was to take charge of their new ship, the Bass Rock, sailing in two days' time from Southampton. He lived at Sydenham, but he was likely to be in that morning for instructions, if we cared to wait for him.

No, Mr. Holmes had no desire to see him, but would be glad to know more about his record and character.

His record was magnificent. There was not an officer in the fleet to touch him. As to his character, he was reliable on duty, but a wild, desperate fellow off the deck of his ship—hot-headed, excitable, but loyal, honest, and kind-hearted. That was the pith of the information with which Holmes left the office of the Adelaide-Southampton company. Thence he drove to Scotland Yard, but, instead of entering, he sat in his cab with his brows drawn down, lost in profound thought. Finally he drove round to the Charing Cross telegraph office, sent off a message, and then, at last, we made for Baker Street once more.

'No, I couldn't do it, Watson,' said he, as we re-entered our room. 'Once that warrant was made out, nothing on earth would save him. Once or twice in my career I feel that I have done more real harm by my discovery of the criminal than ever he had done by his crime. I have learned caution now, and I had rather play tricks with the law of England than with my own conscience. Let us know a little more before We act.'

Before evening, we had a visit from Inspector Stanley Hopkins. Things were not going very well with him.

'I believe that you are a wizard, Mr. Holmes. I really do sometimes think that you have powers that are not human. Now, how on earth could you know that the stolen silver was at the bottom of that pond?'

'I didn't know it.'

'But you told me to examine it.'

'You got it, then?'

'Yes, I got it.'

'I am very glad if I have helped you.'

'But you haven't helped me. You have made the affair far more difficult. What sort of burglars are they who steal silver and then throw it into the nearest pond?'

'It was certainly rather eccentric behaviour. I was merely going on the idea that if the silver had been taken by persons who did not want it—who merely took it for a blind, as it were—then they would naturally be anxious to get rid of it.'

'But why should such an idea cross your mind?'

'Well, I thought it was possible. When they came out through the French window, there was the pond with one tempting little hole in the ice, right in front of their noses. Could there be a better hiding-place?'

'Ah, a hiding-place—that is better!' cried Stanley Hopkins. 'Yes, yes, I see it all now! It was early, there were folk upon the roads, they were afraid of being seen with the silver, so they sank it in the pond, intending to return for it when the coast was clear. Excellent, Mr. Holmes—that is better than your idea of a blind.'

'Quite so, you have got an admirable theory. I have no doubt that my own ideas were quite wild, but you must admit that they have ended in discovering the silver.'

'Yes, sir—yes. It was all your doing. But I have had a bad setback.'

'A setback?'

'Yes, Mr. Holmes. The Randall gang were arrested in New York this morning.'

'Dear me, Hopkins! That is certainly rather against your theory that they committed a murder in Kent last night.'

'It is fatal, Mr. Holmes—absolutely fatal. Still, there are other gangs of three besides the Randalls, or it may be some new gang of which the police have never heard,'

'Quite so, it is perfectly possible. What, are you off?'

'Yes, Mr. Holmes, there is no rest for me until I have got to the bottom of the business. I suppose you have no hint to give me?'

'I have given you one.'

'Which?'

'Well, I suggested a blind.'

'But why, Mr. Holmes, why?'

'Ah, that's the question, of course. But I commend the idea to your mind. You might possibly find that there was something in it. You won't stop for dinner? Well, goodbye, and let us know how you get on.'

Dinner was over, and the table cleared before Holmes alluded to the matter again. He had lit his pipe and held his slippered feet to the cheerful blaze of the fire. Suddenly he looked at his watch.

'I expect developments, Watson.'

'When?'

'Now—within a few minutes. I dare say you thought I acted rather badly to Stanley Hopkins just now.'

'I trust your judgment.'

'A very sensible reply, Watson. You must look at it this way: what I know is unofficial, what he knows is official. I have the right to private judgment, but he has none. He must disclose all, or he is a traitor to his service. In a doubtful case I would not put him in so painful a position, and so I reserve my information until my own mind is clear upon the matter.'

'But when will that be?'

'The time has come. You will now be present at the last scene of a remarkable little drama.'

There was a sound upon the stairs, and our door was opened to admit as fine a specimen of manhood as ever passed through it. He was a very tall young man, golden-moustached, blue-eyed, with a skin which had been burned by tropical suns, and a springy step, which showed that the huge frame was as active as it was strong. He closed the door behind him, and then he stood with clenched hands and heaving breast, choking down some overmastering emotion.

'Sit down, Captain Crocker. You got my telegram?'

Our visitor sank into an armchair and looked from one to the other of us with questioning eyes.

'I got your telegram, and I came at the hour you said. I heard that you had been down to the office. There was no getting away from you. Let's hear the worst. What are you going to do with me? Arrest me? Speak out, man! You can't sit there and play with me like a cat with a mouse.'

'Give him a cigar,' said Holmes. 'Bite on that, Captain Crocker, and don't let your nerves run away with you. I should not sit here smoking with you if I thought that you were a common criminal, you may be sure of that. Be frank with me and we may do some good. Play tricks with me, and I'll crush you.'

'What do you wish me to do?'

To give me a true account of all that happened at the Abbey Grange last night—a true account, mind you, with nothing added and nothing taken off. I know so much already that if you go one inch off the straight, I'll blow this police whistle from my window and the affair goes out of my hands forever.'

The sailor thought for a little. Then he struck his leg with his great sunburned hand.

'I'll chance it,' he cried. 'I believe you are a man of your word, and a white man, and I'll tell you the whole story. But one thing I will say first. So far as I am concerned, I regret nothing and I fear nothing, and I would do it all again and be proud of the job. Damn the beast, if he had as many lives as a cat, he would owe them all to me! But it's the lady, Mary—Mary Fraser—for never will I call her by that accursed name. When I think of getting her into trouble, I who would give my life just to bring one smile to her dear face, it's that that turns my soul into water. And yet—and yet—what less could I do? I'll tell you my story gentlemen, and then I'll ask you, as man to man, what less could I do?

'I must go back a bit. You seem to know everything, so I expect that you know that I met her when she was a passenger and I was first officer of the Rock of Gibraltar. From the first day I met her, she was the only woman to me. Every day of that voyage I loved her more, and many a time since have I kneeled down in the darkness of the night watch and kissed the deck of that ship because I knew her dear feet had trod it. She was never engaged to me. She treated me as fairly as ever a woman treated a man. I have no complaint to make. It was all love on my side, and all good comradeship and friendship on hers. When we parted she was a free woman, but I could never again be a free man.

'Next time I came back from sea, I heard of her marriage. Well, why shouldn't she marry whom she liked? Title and money—who could carry them better than she? She was born for all that is beautiful and dainty. I didn't grieve over her marriage. I was not such a selfish hound as that. I just rejoiced that good luck had come her way, and that she had not thrown herself away on a penniless sailor. That's how I loved Mary Fraser.

'Well, I never thought to see her again, but last voyage I was promoted, and the new boat was not yet launched, so I had to wait for a couple of months with my people at Sydenham. One day out in a country lane I met Theresa Wright, her old maid. She told me all about her, about him, about everything. I tell you, gentlemen, it nearly drove me mad. This drunken hound, that he should dare to raise his hand to her, whose boots he was not worthy to lick! I met Theresa again. Then I met Mary herself—and met her again. Then she would meet me no more. But the other day I had a notice that I was to start on my voyage within a week, and I determined that I would see her once before I left. Theresa was always my friend, for she loved Mary and hated this villain almost as much as I did. From her I learned the ways of the house. Mary used to sit up reading in her own little room downstairs. I crept round there last night and scratched at the window. At first she would not open to me, but in her heart I know that now she loves me, and she could not leave me in the frosty night. She whispered to me to come round to the big front window, and I found it open before me, so as to let me into the dining-room. Again I heard from her own lips things that made my blood boil, and again I cursed this brute who mishandled the woman I loved. Well, gentlemen, I was standing with her just inside the window, in all innocence, as God is my judge, when he rushed like a madman into the room, called her the vilest name that a man could use to a woman, and welted her across the face with the stick he had in his hand. I had sprung for the poker, and it was a fair fight between us. See here, on my arm, where his first blow fell. Then it was my turn, and I went through him as if he had been a rotten pumpkin. Do you think I was sorry? Not I! It was his life or mine, but far more than that, it was his life or hers, for how could I leave her in the power of this madman? That was how I killed him. Was I wrong? well, then, what would either of you gentlemen have done, if you had been in my position?

'She had screamed when he struck her, and that brought old Theresa down from the room above. There was a bottle of wine on the sideboard, and I opened it and poured a little between Mary's lips, for she was half dead with shock. Then I took a drop myself. Theresa was as cool as ice, and it was her plot as much as mine. We must make it appear that burglars had done the thing. Theresa kept on repeating our story to her mistress, while I swarmed up and cut the rope of the bell. Then I lashed her in her chair, and frayed out the end of the rope to make it look natural, else they would wonder how in the world a burglar could have got up there to cut it. Then I gathered up a few plates and pots of silver, to carry out the idea of the robbery, and there I left them, with orders to give the alarm when I had a quarter of an hour's start. I dropped the silver into the pond, and made off for Sydenham, feeling that for once in my life I had done a real good night's work. And that's the truth and the whole truth, Mr. Holmes, if it costs me my neck.'

Holmes smoked for some time in silence. Then he crossed the room, and shook our visitor by the hand.

'That's what I think,' said he. 'I know that every word is true, for you have hardly said a word which I did not know. No one but an acrobat or a sailor could have got up to that bell-rope from the bracket, and no one but a sailor could have made the knots with which the cord was fastened to the chair. Only once had this lady been brought into contact with sailors, and that was on her voyage, and it was someone of her own class of life, since she was trying hard to shield him, and so showing that she loved him. You see how easy it was for me to lay my hands upon you when once I started upon the right trail.'

'I thought the police never could have seen through our dodge.'

'And the police haven't, nor will they, to the best of my belief. Now, look here, Captain Crocker, this is a very serious matter, though I am willing to admit that you acted under the most extreme provocation to which any man could be subjected. I am not sure that in defence of your own life your action will not be pronounced legitimate. However, that is for a British jury to decide. Meanwhile I have so much sympathy for you that, if you choose to disappear in the next twenty-four hours, I will promise you that no one will hinder you.'

'And then it will all come out?'

'Certainly it will come out.'

The sailor flushed with anger.

'What sort of proposal is that to make a man? I know enough of law to understand that Mary would be held as accomplice. Do you think I would leave her alone to face the music while I slunk away? No, sir, let them do their worst upon me, but for heaven's sake, Mr. Holmes, find some way of keeping my poor Mary out of the courts.'

Holmes for a second time held out his hand to the sailor.

'I was only testing you, and you ring true every time. Well, it is a great responsibility that I take upon myself, but I have given Hopkins an excellent hint, and if he can't avail himself of it I can do no more. See here, Captain Crocker, we'll do this in due form of law. You are the prisoner. Watson, you are a British jury, and I never met a man who was more eminently fitted to represent one. I am the judge. Now, gentleman of the jury, you have heard the evidence. Do you find the prisoner guilty or not guilty?'

'Not guilty, my lord,' said I.

'Vox populi, vox Dei. You are acquitted, Captain Crocker. So long as the law does not find some other victim you are safe from me. Come back to this lady in a year, and may her future and yours justify us in the judgment which we have pronounced this night!'

THE PRIZE LODGER
By George Gissing

(Human Odds and Ends/Stories and Sketches, London: Lawrence and Bullen Ltd, 1898)

The ordinary West-End Londoner—who is a citizen of no city at all, but dwells amid a mere conglomerate of houses at a certain distance from Charing Cross—has known a fleeting surprise when, by rare chance, his eye fell upon the name of some such newspaper as the Battersea Times, the Camberwell Mercury, or the Islington Gazette. To him, these and the like districts are nothing more than compass points of the huge metropolis. He may be in practice acquainted with them; if historically inclined, he may think of them as old-time villages swallowed up by insatiable London; but he has never grasped the fact that in Battersea, Camberwell, Islington, there are people living who name these places as their home; who are born, subsist, and die there as though in a distinct town, and practically without consciousness of its obliteration in the map of a world capital.

The stable element of this population consists of more or less old-fashioned people. Round about them is the ceaseless coming and going of nomads who keep abreast with the time, who take their lodgings by the week, their houses by the month; who camp indifferently in regions old and new, learning their geography in train and tram-car. Abiding parishioners are wont to be either very poor or established in a moderate prosperity; they lack enterprise, either for good or ill: if comfortably off, they owe it, as a rule, to some predecessor's exertion. And for the most part, though little enough endowed with the civic spirit, they abundantly pride themselves on their local permanence.

Representative of this class was Mr. Archibald Jordan, a native of Islington, and, at the age of five-and-forty, still faithful to the streets which he had trodden as a child. His father started a small grocery business in Upper Street; Archibald succeeded to the shop, advanced soberly, and at length admitted a partner, by whose capital and energy the business was much increased. After his thirtieth year Mr. Jordan ceased to stand behind the counter. Of no very active disposition, and but moderately set on gain, he found it pleasant to spend a few hours daily over the books and the correspondence, and for the rest of his time to enjoy a gossipy leisure, straying among the acquaintances of a lifetime, or making new in the decorous bar-parlours, billiard-rooms, and other such retreats which allured his bachelor liberty. His dress and bearing were unpretentious, but impressively respectable; he never allowed his garments (made by an Islington tailor, an old schoolfellow) to exhibit the least sign of wear, but fashion affected their style as little as possible. Of middle height, and tending to portliness, he walked at an unvarying pace, as a man who had never known undignified hurry; in his familiar thoroughfares he glanced about him with a good-humoured air of proprietorship, or with a look of thoughtful criticism for any changes that might be going forward. No one had ever spoken flatteringly of his visage; he knew himself a very homely-featured man, and accepted the fact, as something that had neither favoured nor hindered him in life. But it was his conviction that no man's eye had a greater power of solemn and overwhelming rebuke, and this gift he took a pleasure in exercising, however trivial the occasion.

For five-and-twenty years he had lived in lodgings; always within the narrow range of Islington respectability, yet never for more than a twelvemonth under the same roof. This peculiar feature of Mr. Jordan's life had made him a subject of continual interest to local landladies, among whom were several lifelong residents, on friendly terms of old time with the Jordan family.

To them it seemed an astonishing thing that a man in such circumstances had not yet married; granting this eccentricity, they could not imagine what made him change his abode so often. Not a landlady in Islington but would welcome Mr. Jordan in her rooms, and, having got him, do her utmost to prolong the connection. He had been known to quit a house on the paltriest excuse, removing to another in which he could not expect equally good treatment. There was no accounting for it: it must be taken as an ultimate mystery of life, and made the most of as a perennial topic of neighbourly conversation.

As to the desirability of having Mr. Jordan for a lodger there could be no difference of opinion among rational womankind. Mrs. Wiggins, indeed, had taken his sudden departure from her house so ill that she always spoke of him abusively; but who heeded Mrs. Wiggins? Even in the sadness of hope deferred, those ladies who had entertained him once, and speculated on his possible return, declared Mr. Jordan a 'thorough gentleman'. Lodgers, as a class, do not recommend themselves in Islington; Mr. Jordan shone against the dusky background with almost dazzling splendour. To speak of lodgers as of cattle, he was a prize creature. A certain degree of comfort he firmly exacted; he might be a trifle fastidious about cooking; he stood upon his dignity; but no one could say that he grudged reward for service rendered. It was his practice to pay more than the landlady asked. Twenty-five shillings a week, you say? I shall give you twenty-eight. But—' and with raised forefinger he went through the catalogue of his demands. Everything must be done precisely as he directed; even in the laying of his table he insisted upon certain minute peculiarities, and to forget one of them was to earn that gaze of awful reprimand which Mr. Jordan found (or thought) more efficacious than any spoken word. Against this precision might be set his strange indulgence in the matter of bills; he merely regarded the total, was never known to dispute an item. Only twice in his long experience had he quitted a lodging because of exorbitant charges, and on these occasions he sternly refused to discuss the matter. 'Mrs. Hawker, I am paying your account with the addition of one week's rent. Your rooms will be vacant at eleven o'clock tomorrow morning.' And until the hour of departure no entreaty, no prostration, could induce him to utter a syllable.

It was on the 1st of June, 1889, his forty-fifth birthday, that Mr. Jordan removed from quarters he had occupied for ten months, and became a lodger in the house of Mrs. Elderfield.

Mrs. Elderfield, a widow, aged three-and-thirty, with one little girl, was but a casual resident in Islington; she knew nothing of Mr. Jordan, and made no inquiries about him. Strongly impressed, as every woman must needs be, by his air and tone of mild authority, she congratulated herself on the arrival of such an inmate; but no subservience appeared in her demeanour; she behaved with studious civility, nothing more. Her words were few and well chosen. Always neatly dressed, yet always busy, she moved about the house with quick, silent step, and cleanliness marked her path. The meals were well cooked, well served. Mr. Jordan being her only lodger, she could devote to him an undivided attention. At the end of his first week the critical gentleman felt greater satisfaction than he had ever known.

The bill lay upon his table at breakfast-time. He perused the items, and, much against his habit, reflected upon them. Having breakfasted, he rang the bell.

'Mrs. Elderfield—'

He paused, and looked gravely at the widow. She had a plain, honest, healthy face, with resolute lips, and an eye that brightened when she spoke; her well-knit figure, motionless in its respectful attitude, declared a thoroughly sound condition of the nerves.

'Mrs. Elderfield, your bill is so very moderate that I think you must have forgotten something.'

'Have you looked it over, sir?'

'I never trouble with the details. Please examine it.'

'There is no need, sir. I never make a mistake.'

'I said, Mrs. Elderfield, please examine it.'

She seemed to hesitate, but obeyed.

'The bill is quite correct, sir.'

'Thank you.'

He paid it at once and said no more.

The weeks went on. To Mr. Jordan's surprise, his landlady's zeal and efficiency showed no diminution, a thing unprecedented in his long and varied experience. After the first day or two he had found nothing to correct; every smallest instruction was faithfully carried out. Moreover, he knew for the first time in his life the comfort of absolutely clean rooms. The best of his landladies hitherto had not risen above that conception of cleanliness which is relative to London soot and fog. His palate, too, was receiving an education. Probably he had never eaten of a joint rightly cooked, or tasted a potato boiled as it should be; more often than not, the food set before him had undergone a process which left it masticable indeed, but void of savour and nourishment. Many little attentions of which he had never dreamed kept him in a wondering cheerfulness. And at length he said to himself: 'Here I shall stay.'

Not that his constant removals had been solely due to discomfort and a hope of better things. The secret—perhaps not entirely revealed even to himself—lay in Mr. Jordan's sense of his own importance, and his uneasiness whenever he felt that, in the eyes of a landlady, he was becoming a mere everyday person—an ordinary lodger. No sooner did he detect a sign of this than he made up his mind to move. It gave him the keenest pleasure of which he was capable when, on abruptly announcing his immediate departure, he perceived the landlady's profound mortification. To make the blow heavier he had even resorted to artifice, seeming to express a most lively contentment during the very days when he had decided to leave and was asking himself where he should next abide. One of his delights was to return to a house which he had quitted years ago, to behold the excitement and bustle occasioned by his appearance, and play the good-natured autocrat over grovelling dependents. In every case, save the two already mentioned, he had parted with his landlady on terms of friendliness, never vouchsafing a reason for his going away, genially eluding every attempt to obtain an explanation, and at the last abounding in graceful recognition of all that had been done for him. Mr. Jordan shrank from dispute, hated every sort of contention; this characteristic gave a certain refinement to his otherwise commonplace existence. Vulgar vanity would have displayed itself in precisely the acts and words from which his self-esteem nervously shrank. And of late he had been thinking over the list of landladies, with a half-formed desire to settle down, to make himself a permanent home. Doubtless as a result of this state of mind, he betook himself to a strange house, where, as from neutral ground, he might reflect upon the lodgings he knew, and judge between their merits. He could not foresee what awaited him under Mrs. Elderfield's roof; the event impressed him as providential; he felt, with singular emotion, that choice was taken out of his hands. Lodgings could not be more than perfect, and such he had found.

It was not his habit to chat with landladies. At times he held forth to them on some topic of interest, suavely, instructively; if he gave in to their ordinary talk, it was with a half-absent smile of condescension. Mrs. Elderfield seeming as little disposed to gossip as himself, a month elapsed before he knew anything of her history; but one evening the reserve on both sides was broken. His landlady modestly inquired whether she was giving satisfaction, and Mr. Jordan replied with altogether unwonted fervour. In the dialogue that ensued, they exchanged personal confidences. The widow had lost her husband four years ago; she came from the Midlands, but had long dwelt in London. Then fell from her lips a casual remark which made the hearer uneasy.

'I don't think I shall always stay here. The neighbourhood is too crowded. I should like to have a house somewhere further out.'

Mr. Jordan did not comment on this, but it kept a place in his daily thoughts, and became at length so much of an anxiety that he invited a renewal of the subject.

'You have no intention of moving just yet, Mrs. Elderfield?'

'I was going to tell you, sir,' replied the landlady, with her respectful calm, 'that I have decided to make a change next spring. Some friends of mine have gone to live at Wood Green, and I shall look for a house in the same neighbourhood.'

Mr. Jordan was, in private, gravely disturbed. He who had flitted from house to house for many years, distressing the souls of landladies, now lamented the prospect of a forced removal. It was open to him to accompany Mrs. Elderfield, but he shrank from the thought of living in so remote a district. Wood Green! The very name appalled him, for he had never been able to endure the country. He betook himself one dreary autumn afternoon to that northern suburb, and what he saw did not at all reassure him. On his way back he began once more to review the list of old lodgings.

But from that day his conversations with Mrs. Elderfield grew more frequent, more intimate. In the evening he occasionally made an excuse for knocking at her parlour door, and lingered for a talk which ended only at supper time. He spoke of his own affairs, and grew more ready to do so as his hearer manifested a genuine interest, without impertinent curiosity. Little by little he imparted to Mrs. Elderfield a complete knowledge of his commercial history, of his pecuniary standing—matters of which he had never before spoken to a mere acquaintance. A change was coming over him; the foundations of habit crumbled beneath his feet; he lost his look of complacence, his self-confident and superior tone. Bar-parlours and billiard-rooms saw him but rarely and flittingly. He seemed to have lost his pleasure in the streets of Islington, and spent all his spare time by the fireside, perpetually musing.

On a day in March one of his old landladies, Mrs. Higdon, sped to the house of another, Mrs. Evans, panting under a burden of strange news. Could it be believed! Mr. Jordan was going to marry—to marry that woman in whose house he was living! Mrs. Higdon had it on the very best authority—that of Mr. Jordan's partner, who spoke of the affair without reserve. A new house had already been taken—at Wood Green. Well! After all these years, after so many excellent opportunities, to marry a mere stranger and forsake Islington! In a moment Mr. Jordan's character was gone; had he figured in the police-court under some disgraceful charge, these landladies could hardly have felt more shocked and professed themselves more disgusted. The intelligence spread. Women went out of their way to have a sight of Mrs. Elderfield's house; they hung about for a glimpse of that sinister person herself. She had robbed them, every one, of a possible share in Islington's prize lodger. Had it been one of themselves they could have borne the chagrin; but a woman whom not one of them knew, an alien! What base arts had she practised? Ah, it was better not to inquire too closely into the secrets of that lodging-house.

Though every effort was made to learn the time and place of the ceremony, Mr. Jordan's landladies had the mortification to hear of his wedding only when it was over. Of course, this showed that he felt the disgracefulness of his behaviour; he was not utterly lost to shame. It could only be hoped that he would not know the bitterness of repentance.

Not till he found himself actually living in the house at Wood Green did Mr. Jordan realize how little his own will had had to do with the recent course of events. Certainly, he had made love to the widow, and had asked her to marry him; but from that point onward he seemed to have put himself entirely in Mrs. Elderfield's hands, granting every request, meeting half-way every suggestion she offered, becoming, in short, quite a different kind of man from his former self. He had not been sensible of a moment's reluctance; he enjoyed the novel sense of yielding himself to affectionate guidance. His wits had gone wool-gathering; they returned to him only after the short honeymoon at Brighton, when he stood upon his own hearth-rug, and looked round at the new furniture and ornaments which symbolized a new beginning of life.

The admirable landlady had shown herself energetic, clear-headed, and full of resource; it was she who chose the house, and transacted all the business in connection with it; Mr. Jordan had merely run about in her company from place to place, smiling approval and signing cheques. No one could have gone to work more prudently, or obtained what she wanted at smaller outlay; for all that, Mr. Jordan, having recovered something like his normal frame of mind, viewed the results with consternation. Left to himself, he would have taken a very small house, and furnished it much in the style of Islington lodgings; as it was, he occupied a ten-roomed 'villa', with appointments which seemed to him luxurious, aristocratic. True, the expenditure was of no moment to a man in his position, and there was no fear that Mrs. Jordan would involve him in dangerous extravagance; but he had always lived with such excessive economy that the sudden change to a life correspondent with his income could not but make him uncomfortable.

Mrs. Jordan had, of course, seen to it that her personal appearance harmonized with the new surroundings. She dressed herself and her young daughter with careful appropriateness. There was no display, no purchase of gewgaws—merely garments of good quality, such as became people in easy circumstances. She impressed upon her husband that this was nothing more than a return to the habits of her earlier life. Her first marriage had been a sad mistake; it had brought her down in the world. Now she felt restored to her natural position.

After a week of restlessness, Mr. Jordan resumed his daily visits to the shop in Upper Street, where he sat as usual among the books and the correspondence, and tried to assure himself that all would henceforth be well with him. No more changing from house to house; a really comfortable home in which to spend the rest of his days; a kind and most capable wife to look after all his needs, to humour all his little habits. He could not have taken a wiser step.

For all that, he had lost something, though he did not yet

understand what it was. The first perception of a change not for the better flashed upon him one evening in the second week, when he came home an hour later than his wont. Mrs. Jordan, who always stood waiting for him at the window, had no smile as he entered.

'Why are you late?' she asked, in her clear, restrained voice.

'Oh—something or other kept me.'

This would not do. Mrs. Jordan quietly insisted on a full explanation of the delay, and it seemed to her unsatisfactory.

'I hope you won't be irregular in your habits, Archibald,' said his wife, with gentle admonition. 'What I always liked in you was your methodical way of living. I shall be very uncomfortable if I never know when to expect you.'

'Yes, my dear, but—business, you see—'

'But you have explained that you could have been back at the usual time.'

'Yes—that's true—but—'

'Well, well, you won't let it happen again. Oh really, Archibald!' she suddenly exclaimed. 'The idea of you coming into the room with muddy boots! Why, look! There's a patch of mud on the carpet—'

'It was my hurry to speak to you,' murmured Mr. Jordan, in confusion.

'Please go at once and take your boots off. And you left your slippers in the bedroom this morning. You must always bring them down, and put them in the dining-room cupboard; then they're ready for you when you come into the house.'

Mr. Jordan had but a moderate appetite for his dinner, and he did not talk so pleasantly as usual. This was but the beginning of troubles such as he had not for a moment foreseen. His wife, having since their engagement taken the upper hand, began to show her determination to keep it, and day by day her rule grew more galling to the ex-bachelor. He himself, in the old days, had plagued his landladies by insisting upon method and routine, by his faddish attention to domestic minutiae; he now learnt what it was to be subjected to the same kind of despotism, exercised with much more exasperating persistence. Whereas Mrs. Elderfield had scrupulously obeyed every direction given by her lodger, Mrs. Jordan was evidently resolved that her husband should live, move, and have his being in the strictest accordance with her own ideal. Not in any spirit of nagging, or ill-tempered unreasonableness; it was merely that she had her favourite way of doing every conceivable thing, and felt so sure it was the best of all possible ways that she could not endure any other. The first serious disagreement between them had reference to conduct at the breakfast-table. After a broken night, feeling headachy and worried, Mr. Jordan took up his newspaper, folded it conveniently, and set it against the bread so that he could read while eating. Without a word, his wife gently removed it, and laid it aside on a chair.

'What are you doing?' he asked gruffly.

'You mustn't read at meals, Archibald. It's bad manners, and bad for your digestion.'

'I've read the news at breakfast all my life, and I shall do so still,' exclaimed the husband, starting up and recovering his paper.

'Then you will have breakfast by yourself. Nelly, we must go into the other room till papa has finished.'

Mr. Jordan ate mechanically, and stared at the newspaper with just as little consciousness. Prompted by the underlying weakness of his character to yield for the sake of peace, wrath made him dogged, and the more steadily he regarded his position, the more was he appalled by the outlook. Why, this meant downright slavery! He had married a woman so horribly like himself in several points that his only hope lay in overcoming her by sheer violence. A thoroughly good and well-meaning woman, an excellent housekeeper, the kind of wife to do him credit and improve his social position; but self-willed, pertinacious, and probably thinking herself his superior in every respect. He had nothing to fear but subjection—the one thing he had never anticipated, the one thing he could never endure.

He went off to business without seeing his wife again, and passed a lamentable day. At his ordinary hour of return, instead of setting off homeward, he strayed about the by-streets of Islington and Pentonville. Not till this moment had he felt how dear they were to him, the familiar streets; their very odours fell sweet upon his nostrils. Never again could he go hither and thither, among the old friends, the old places, to his heart's content. What had possessed him to abandon this precious liberty! The thought of Wood Green revolted him; live there as long as he might, he would never be at home. He thought of his wife (now waiting for him) with fear, and then with a reaction of rage. Let her wait! He—Archibald Jordan—before whom women had bowed and trembled for five-and-twenty years—was he to come and go at a wife's bidding? And at length the thought seemed so utterly preposterous that he sped northward as fast as possible, determined to right himself this very evening.

Mrs. Jordan sat alone. He marched into the room with muddy

boots, flung his hat and overcoat into a chair, and poked the fire violently. His wife's eye was fixed on him, and she first spoke—in the quiet voice that he dreaded.

'What do you mean by carrying on like this, Archibald?'

'I shall carry on as I like in my own house—hear that?'

'I do hear it, and I'm very sorry too. It gives me a very bad opinion of you. You will not do as you like in your own house. Rage as you please. You will not do as you like in your own house.'

There was a contemptuous anger in her eye which the man could not face. He lost all control of himself, uttered coarse oaths, and stood quivering. Then the woman began to lecture him; she talked steadily, acrimoniously, for more than an hour, regardless of his interruptions. Nervously exhausted, he fled at length from the room. A couple of hours later they met again in the nuptial chamber, and again Mrs. Jordan began to talk. Her point, as before, was that he had begun married life about as badly as possible. Why had he married her at all? What fault had she committed to incur such outrageous usage? But, thank goodness, she had a will of her own, and a proper self-respect; behave as he might, she would still persevere in the path of womanly duty. If he thought to make her life unbearable he would find his mistake; she simply should not heed him; perhaps he would return to his senses before long—and in this vein Mrs. Jordan continued until night was at odds with morning, only becoming silent when her partner had sunk into the oblivion of uttermost fatigue.

The next day Mr. Jordan's demeanour showed him, for the moment at all events, defeated. He made no attempt to read at breakfast; he moved about very quietly. And in the afternoon he came home at the regulation hour.

Mrs. Jordan had friends in the neighbourhood, but she saw little of them. She was not a woman of ordinary tastes. Everything proved that, to her mind, the possession of a nice house, with the prospects of a comfortable life, was an end in itself; she had no desire to exhibit her well-furnished rooms, or to gad about talking of her advantages. Every moment of her day was taken up in the superintendence of servants, the discharge of an infinitude of housewifely tasks. She had no assistance from her daughter; the girl went to school, and was encouraged to study with the utmost application. The husband's presence in the house seemed a mere accident—save in the still nocturnal season, when Mrs. Jordan bestowed upon him her counsel and her admonitions.

After the lapse of a few days Mr. Jordan again offered combat, and threw himself into it with a frenzy.

'Look here!' he shouted at length, 'either you or I are going to leave this house. I can't live with you—understand? I hate the sight of you!'

'Go on!' retorted the other, with mild bitterness. 'Abuse me as much as you like, I can bear it. I shall continue to do my duty, and unless you have recourse to personal violence, here I remain. If you go too far, of course the law must defend me!'

This was precisely what Mr. Jordan knew and dreaded; the law was on his wife's side, and by applying at a police-court for protection she could overwhelm him with shame and ridicule, which would make life intolerable. Impossible to argue with this woman. Say what he might, the fault always seemed his. His wife was simply doing her duty—in a spirit of admirable thoroughness; he, in the eyes of a third person, would appear an unreasonable and violent curmudgeon. Had it not all sprung out of his obstinacy with regard to reading at breakfast? How explain to anyone what he suffered in his nerves, in his pride, in the outraged habitudes of a lifetime?

That evening he did not return to Wood Green. Afraid of questions if he showed himself in the old resorts, he spent some hours in a billiard-room near King's Cross, and towards midnight took a bedroom under the same roof. On going to business next day, he awaited with tremors either a telegram or a visit from his wife; but the whole day passed, and he heard nothing. After dark he walked once more about the beloved streets, pausing now and then to look up at the windows of this or that well remembered house. Ah, if he durst but enter and engage a lodging! Impossible—for ever impossible!

He slept in the same place as on the night before. And again a day passed without any sort of inquiry from Wood Green. When evening came he went home.

Mrs. Jordan behaved as though he had returned from business in the usual way. 'Is it raining?' she asked, with a half-smile. And her husband replied, in as matter-of-fact a tone as he could command, 'No, it isn't.' There was no mention between them of his absence. That night, Mrs. Jordan talked for an hour or two of his bad habit of stepping on the paint when he went up and down stairs, then fell calmly asleep.

But Mr. Jordan did not sleep for a long time. What! was he, after all, to be allowed his liberty out of doors, provided he relinquished it within? Was it really the case that his wife, satisfied with her house and furniture and income, did not care a jot whether he stayed away or came home? There, indeed, gleamed a hope. When Mr. Jordan slept, he dreamed that he was back again in lodgings at Islington, tasting an extraordinary bliss. Day dissipated the vision, but still Mrs. Jordan spoke not a word of his absence, and with trembling still he hoped.

www.ingramcontent.com/pod-product-compliance
Lightning Source LLC
Chambersburg PA
CBHW010400310726
48979CB00017B/2795/J

* 9 7 8 1 6 4 7 9 9 9 4 6 9 *